Joseph Skipsey

The Poems, with Specimens of the Prose Writings, of William Blake

With a Prefatory Notice, Biographical and Critical

Joseph Skipsey

The Poems, with Specimens of the Prose Writings, of William Blake
With a Prefatory Notice, Biographical and Critical

ISBN/EAN: 9783744772730

Printed in Europe, USA, Canada, Australia, Japan

Cover: Foto ©Andreas Hilbeck / pixelio.de

More available books at **www.hansebooks.com**

THE POEMS,

WITH SPECIMENS OF THE PROSE WRITINGS,

OF

WILLIAM BLAKE.

With a Prefatory Notice, Biographical and Critical.

BY

JOSEPH SKIPSEY.

London:
WALTER SCOTT, 14 PATERNOSTER SQUARE,
AND NEWCASTLE-ON-TYNE.
1885.

The Canterbury Poets.

NEW EDITION OF THE POETS.

Edited by JOSEPH SKIPSEY, Author of "Lyric Poems."

In Shilling Monthly Volumes. Each Volume will contain 288 *pages, including an original Introductory Notice, biographical and critical, by various Contributors. Volumes already issued*—COLERIDGE, SHELLEY, LONGFELLOW, BLAKE, *followed by* CAMPBELL, POE, WORDSWORTH, CHATTERTON, MARLOWE, MILTON, WHITTIER, KEBLE, BURNS (2 *vols.*), HERBERT, KEATS, TANNAHILL, BRYANT, COWPER, SCOTT, *etc.*

A FEW OPINIONS OF THE PRESS.

"Well printed on good paper, and nicely bound."—*The Athenæum.*

"Altogether, the volumes are of a convenient size and agreeable appearance."—*Spectator.*

"The first volume of a new series which bids fair to be a popular one. Cheap but excellent edition."—*Literary World.*

"Publisher, printer, and editor all round may be fairly congratulated upon an undoubted success."—*The English Household Magazine.*

"Is emphatically one of the best things in cheap literature which has yet seen the light."—*Brighton Guardian.*

"Clearness of type, handiness in size, and general elegance."—*Dundee Advertiser.*

"A pretty little book, beautifully printed."—*Newcastle Daily Journal.*

"The reasonable price will make this edition most popular."—*Northern Leader.*

"Very pretty and appetising. Sure to be popular."—*Cambridge Independent.*

LONDON : WALTER SCOTT, 14 PATERNOSTER SQUARE.

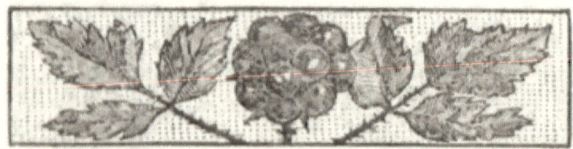

CONTENTS.

Introductory Sketch.

HE remarkable poet-artist, whose poems we here submit to public attention, William Blake, was born on the 28th of November 1757, at 28 Broad Street, Carnaby Market, Golden Square, London. His father was a hosier in poor circumstances, and this may help to account for the neglect of his early education; for all his knowledge, according to Mr Gilchrist, from whose precious and admirable book on Blake we draw the few biographic facts we are about to give, beyond that of reading and writing, was evidently self-acquired

knowledge. From this lack of early discipline to some extent may be ascribed the premature development of his marvellous imaginative faculty—his somewhat powerful self-assertive spirit—and his early dalliance with the muses ; for he was scarcely out of the years of infancy before he began to write verse, and one of the very loveliest lyrics in the English tongue was produced by Blake before he was fourteen years old. It is merely entitled " A Song," and runs thus—

> " How sweet I roamed from field to field
>   And tasted all the summer's pride,
> Till I the Prince of Love beheld,
>   Who in the sunny beams did glide !
>
> " He showed me lilies for my hair,
>   And blushing roses for my brow ;
> He led me through his garden fair,
>   Where all his golden pleasures grow.
>
> " With sweet May-dews my wings are wet,
>   And Phœbus fired my vocal rage ;
> He caught me in his silken net,
>   And shut me in his golden cage.

" He loves to sit and hear me sing,
    Then, laughing, sports and plays with me ;
Then stretches out my golden wing,
    And mocks my loss of liberty."

Talk of inspiration !—if the boy who produced that was not inspired, then who in any age ever was ?   For airiness, brightness, and suggestiveness, we have only a very few such lyrics ; but it is remarkable that one of those few was also produced by another " marvellous boy " at about the same age that the hosier's son was when he produced this. The poem referred to is entitled " To Helen," and its writer was Edgar Allan Poe; and as it may be interesting to the reader to have this other jewel at hand for the sake of comparison, we here subjoin it—

SONG TO HELEN.

" Helen, thy beauty is to me
    Like those Nicean barks of yore,
That gently o'er a perfumed sea
    The weary, way-worn wanderer bore
    To his own native shore.

> " On desperate seas long wont to roam,
>   Thy hyacinth hair, thy classic face,
> Thy Naiad airs have brought me home
>   To the glory that was Greece,
>   And the grandeur that was Rome.

> " Lo, in yon brilliant window niche
>   How statue-like I see thee stand,
>   The agate lamp within thy hand ;
> Ah, Psyche from the regions which
>   Are holy-land !"

At the age of ten our poet-artist attended a drawing school in the Strand, and at the age of fourteen he was sent as an apprentice to an engraver, a Mr. James Basire (evidently of foreign origin), in Great Queen Street, Lincoln's Inn Fields. It is pleasant to think that while yet a boy, in his position of apprentice to an engraver, he would be brought into contact with notable people, and that he once at least did, at his master's shop, see the sweet-souled author of the *Vicar of Wakefield*, " whose finely marked head " he gazed at, and " thought to himself how much he should like to have such a head when he grew to be a man."

Mr. Allingham supposes that also about the same time he may unwittingly often have met in the street, or have walked beside, "a placid, thin man of eighty-four, of erect figure and abstracted air," the greatest of modern vision-seers, "Emanuel Swedenborg, then upon a visit to England." I venture to say that had those two wonderful beings so met, though they might not have known each other by name, they would, none the less—notwithstanding the fact that in after days, from some mysterious cause, the younger underrated the elder—have mutually hailed in each other a kindred genius, and somehow the piercing glance of the Swedish seer would have gone down into the upturned eyes of the filled-with-wonderment boy poet-artist, and a sensation would have passed through their souls that would have been remembered till the day of their death. Men of genius have an unerring instinct for the detection of genius in others, and Blake had also the ever-attendant qualities of the highest genius, and eyes less penetrating than those of the great seer would naturally be kindly drawn to young Blake, for the open-heartedness and utter guilelessness of the boy, I imagine, was such as to be felt by all who came into contact with him ; and it is gratifying to find upon record that his master, Mr. Basire himself, was among those who felt and appreciated these noble qualities in his apprentice, as it is to find that the apprentice, all through his fairly long life, retained and cherished an affection and admiration for his kind-hearted master.

About two years after he had been bound, Mr. Basire, who must have had the utmost confidence in his drawing ability as well as in his truthfulness and honesty, sent him (to be out of harm's way—the danger of suffering from the company of other of his apprentices, of whom the good master had not so high an opinion) into Westminster Abbey and the various old churches in and near London, to make drawings from the monuments and buildings for a work he was engaged to engrave. This would undoubtedly exert a powerful influence upon his tastes and habits, as Mr. Gilchrist intimates, and "have been singularly adapted to foster the romantic turn of his imagination, and to strengthen his affinities for the spiritual in art," and more especially, I would add, for the spiritual in poetry, of which he had already produced the delightful specimen before cited.

On the expiration of his apprenticeship he went to study at the Royal Academy, then yet in its infancy, where he extended his acquaint· anceship among artists, and soon ranked among his friends and appreciators, Stothard, Flaxman, and afterwards Fuseli—the two last named of whom set the highest value on his art genius; while Flaxman, at the same time, declared his genius for poetry to be as great as that he possessed for art. Fuseli, who, at the time of Blake's introduction to him, was in the height of his popularity, continued his friend and champion to the end; and Flaxman, with the exception of a brief period during which an unhappy misunderstanding existed between them, was also a life-long friend and defender —and friends and defenders from the earliest stages of his poetic and artistic career our poet-artist unhappily needed.

In his twenty-fifth year, on a Sunday, the 18th day of August in 1782, Blake was married at Battersea to Catherine Boucher, who was ordained to be throughout the years of his manhood and old age, into which the sun of fortune seldom or never threw a heart-cheering beam, a most precious helpmate. Catherine, like himself, was poor, and of poor parents, and without a school education—a cross was affixed to her name in the marriage contract; but she had a capacity for learning, and a desire to learn— the two grand things—and under the tutorage of her husband she soon learned to read and write. She also learned to print his engravings and how to colour; and having opened an engraver's shop, we are told that she became his saleswoman. Nay, into whatever scheme for the furtherance of his art or the betterment of his condition, or for the gratification, as it might to the non-initiated appear, of some mere fantastic whim, he entered into, she too entered, and clearly with her whole heart and soul. Never was a man of genius blessed with such a woman for a wife as this same little dark-eyed Catherine Boucher proved to William Blake. Nay, I ought to say that never was a common-minded man, dullard, or dunce, so blessed—for it would seem to be written in the fate of men of genius that they should have the most

B

unsuitable women for wives, as from the days of "Athena's wisest son," the immortal and ever beloved Socrates and his Xantippe, the private lives of the most gifted sons of fame in all nations would appear to testify. In our nation—to mention a few—Dickens and his wife, Bulwer Lytton and his wife, Sterne and his wife, Byron and his wife, as is well known, lived all discordant lives—and even the divine Milton had his matrimonial troubles. Of course the women in most of these cases were not to blame more than their liege lords—nay, in some cases not so much, and were evidently the greatest sufferers—as in all likelihood was the wife of Byron. Then, what sort of a time must Jean Armour have had of it with poor Burns? or in their early marriage years what must have been that of the beautiful Anne Hathaway with the young Shakespeare, since, as Mr. John Oldcastle observes, "the dark lady with the sallow face and black eyes, which were so beautiful to Shakespeare in spite of the taste of the time, she to whom half of his sonnets were written, whoever she may have been, was not Anne Hathaway." Catherine Boucher was assuredly not altogether without her matrimonial troubles, but these were of a kind totally unakin to those from which Burns's Bonnie Jean must have suffered, and wholly such as would momentarily arise out of the irritability of her husband's temper, and would pass off without leaving any deep stings in her heart, seeing, as she did, that such irritability was in a great measure the result of his neglect by the world—a world to which he must have felt himself to be a herald of a new era in art and song—for such a herald he truly was. Collins and Gray and Chatterton had each, in various degrees it is true, already pointed the way to the realisation of that same era, so far as song went ; but in the lyrics, as well as the designs of Blake, was more pronounced that return,

in the highest and noblest sense, to nature—to
nature as seen through the magic glass of the
imagination—and to which the world to some
extent, through the later born Wordsworth and
Coleridge and Shelley, afterwards should be
aroused; though he, like those who had gone
before, was destined to warble his immortal
songs for the time like a nightingale in the
night, unheard or unheeded. The first song-
proofs to his claim for this praise were put into
print in the *Poetical Sketches* a short time after
his marriage—that is in 1783, when Burns was
only in his twenty-fourth year, and altogether
unknown to fame, when Coleridge was in his
eleventh year, and Wordsworth was in his
thirteenth, and Byron and Shelley and Keats
were as yet unborn, and several of which proofs
—for nearly all the best of the said *Sketches*,
it is surmised, were written between Blake's
twelfth and twentieth years—were produced
fully a decade before that period.

I have said that he sang unheard and un-heeded, and from the first, save by a small knot of devoted friends, he always did, and in con-sequence the *Poetical Sketches* fell still-born from the press; and this would mean, beside the excruciating pangs of disappointment only known to himself, and in a lesser degree to his own dear wife, a money loss to the poor poet which he was little able to sustain. Nor could Blake be said to ever have earned a penny, save through his ability and labours as a designer and engraver; and though on the whole, in the opinion of competent judges, he was ever badly paid even for these, yet he managed to live— was never in a state of misery—was never reduced to pawn his manhood, or his honour, and to leave them, till out of credit, in pawn, as many who have made a mighty deal of more noise in the world than he have done; nor amid all his difficulties, except from the dearest of friends, would he submit to accept a favour,

for he rightly valued his independence as of
more value than rubies and gold. Of course,
his condition at times would seem miserable
enough to those to whom life would be a blank
if they had not a fine house to live in, a fine
carriage to ride in, and all that goes to form the
beau ideal of life to the vulgar mind; but this
man had within him a treasury before which all
such things appeared but gilded toys and
empty nothings—nay, and somewhat worse, for
did he not sing—

> "Since all the riches of this world
>   May be gifts from the devil and earthly kings;
> I should suspect that I worshipped the devil,
>   If I thanked my God for worldly things.
>
> The countless gold of a merry heart,
>   The rubies and pearls of a loving eye,
> The idle man can never bring from the mart,
>   Nor the cunning hoard up in his treasury."

Did he not sing thus? And what did he
sing that did not spring from the depths of his

soul? In 1787 died Robert—a brother of Blake, and five years his junior—which was, without doubt, a severe loss to him, as, being similarly mentally constituted, the two brothers would have been of great service to each other. However this might have been, the love between the brothers was most powerful, and the death was felt in a way that is seldom felt by one brother for the loss of another. Days and nights had the younger, in his illness, been attended and nursed by the elder; and, when the last and most trying moment had arrived, wherein the spirit should be released from its clay bonds, the bereaved poet at least had the consolation—so he believed—of seeing it "ascend," says Mr. Gilchrist, "through the matter-of-fact ceiling" and "clapping its hands for joy!" "No wonder he could paint such scenes;" no wonder, dear reader—and such scenes he did paint, and continued to paint to the end; and with the aid, he would declare, of this very spirit-brother, the loss of whom, through his departure from the flesh, by the-by, I am afraid I have just magnified, since the spirits of the brothers, after this catastrophe, would seem to have become more closely united than ever; and that for the purpose of working out the art and the literary schemes which come to us as the products of William Blake only.

The first fruit of this supposed co-operation of the two minds was the invention of a process by which the poet-artist should be both the printer as well as the illustrator of his own songs. Long before his brother's death a part of a second series of lyrics must have been written of even greater value, upon the whole, than the neglected, but none the less immortal *Poetical Sketches*, and the time had now come when these should appear before the world; but the means—the means—where were the means to be had? for clearly the patronage of a certain blue-stocking circle, which had aided him in his first effort to catch the eye and ear of the reading public, had in that one good deed been exhausted; and how was the printing, not to say the publication, of this second book of songs to be effected? The question was a vexed one, and had strained his faculties to the uttermost, when lo, his departed and deeply deplored brother appeared to him in a vision, and showed him the *how*, by revealing "the wished for secret," and "directing him to the technical mode by which could be produced a fac-simile of song and design;" and a book was the outcome, which was at once written by, illustrated by, and printed and engraved by William Blake. For an exposition of this process the reader must be referred to Mr. Gilchrist's *Blake*, as I am already too much indebted to that fine book to filch this piece of information from its valuable pages, and so shall only here add that such was the way in which the ever delightful

Songs of Innocence, and in which, in sooth, all the Blake-after-work song and design were ushered into the world—that world, in this particular case, being comprised of the few curiosity-hunters who might happen to stray along Poland Street, " the long street which connects Broad Street with Oxford Street," and to which, I suppose, shortly after his brother's death, the poet had removed, for the critics were too much occupied with other and more pretentious issues to take much heed of the poet's modest thin brochure, or to have that passiveness essential to appreciate " the child-angel " pictures or " the child-angel " melodies contained therein. This was in 1788-1789, and six years after appeared the *Songs of Experience,* in which again we have a treasury of the richest jewels, and such as few ever could, beside our poet, produce when he wrote at his best; and in these three issues— *Poetical Sketches, Songs of Innocence,* and *Songs of Experience,* and a few lyrics which were produced at rare intervals in later years, and to which might be added that "strange, mystical allegory," the *Book of Thel*, we have comprised the harvest of our poet's true song; for though he poured forth a multitude of writings—his so-called prophecies— many passages of which are written with absolute sincerity, as Allan Cunningham said of his poems, "with infinite tenderness," and "are in verity the words of a great and wise mind," yet as there is in these, according to those most competent to judge, a lack of organic, not to say a lack of harmonic organic unity, and cannot in any just sense be termed poems, it were folly, and an injury and a drawback to his fame, to persist in classing them with his poems proper. Many of his poems are mystical and enigmatical, but they are nearly all characterised by that exquisite metrical gift, and rightness in point of form and colour, which Dante Rosetti said "constitute Blake's special glory among his contemporaries," but which cannot be said of the *Prophecies*—the *Thel* perhaps excepted. His harvest, I repeat—and a golden one it is—with the exception of the precious ears specified, was reaped in the production of the last-named songs (1794), when our poet was in his thirty-seventh year, and his *Prophecies ;* and, happily, with these his best series of designs, which included his "Canterbury Pilgrims," his "Blair's Grave," and his crowning glory as an artist, his "Designs for the Book of Job," were to be the outcome of the inspiration of his after years.

It is remarkable that the more and more he seemed to become unable to catch the true inspiration of the poet, the more and more, and with a firmer grasp of the pencil, he seemed to be able to catch the true inspiration of the designer, and the question arises, whether the fame of Blake, or, indeed, that of any other genius, however powerful and lofty, was ever aught the better through the cultivation of two arts—whether that fame would not have been sounder, safer, and more universal, had such a genius sought and found a satisfactory expression in one art only, as that of a Homer, a Dante, or a Shakespeare did—as that of a Phidias, a Raphael, or a Handel did; or whether through two or more arts, such as were cultivated and enriched by the genius of a Michael Angelo, a Leonardo De Vinci, or by that of a William Blake, or a Dante Gabriel Rosetti. Much, assuredly, could be said on both sides of this question, but perhaps to small purpose, save as an exercise of the mind; for after all was said that could be said upon the subject, the career of a real genius would remain unaffected by the issue. And the reason is clear. Men of genius are men of genius simply because they are formed with the capacity for the reception into their internals

of a divine power, and when they are caught
up by that power—by the Spirit of Inspiration
—as Ezekiel of old was caught up by the hair
of the head, and hurried through the air, and
placed among the Elders of the ages fled, in
the Temple of Jerusalem, there is no saying in
what trim or in what course they ought to go—
nay, they themselves may have no choice in the
matter. One course only for the moment may
be open, and one goal in view ; and in that
course, and to that goal, must speed " the fiery
chariot of genius," whatever follows ; and if
the course be up into heaven—then good ; and
if down into Jericho, or some other where for
which nobody cares—why, then, also good ; one
vessel, to common observation, being made to
honour and another to dishonour ; but the ways
of the muse are not always scrutable, and if,
under the said divine power, the said goal be
in verity reached, then the poet, or the artist, or
the poet-artist will know that he has done the

right thing, and that right thing through
the right means—and this while under the
said power, inspiration, or soul-illumination,
Michael Angelo, Dante Rosetti, and William
Blake evidently did know. Of course this
leaves the question yet open whether Blake
did not often write, as in those sphinx-like
prophetic books of his, when he was not under
that divine power, and whether he did not
often miss the mark, when, under some wild
freak of fancy instead, he believed he had
reached the desired goal. I for one have
strong doubts thereon, and that notwithstanding
the fact that the highly-gifted Mr. Swinburne
appears to be able to penetrate and to bring to
light the most precious jewels of meaning from
passages in those books, which otherwise are, to
my weaker sight, as dark as a coal-pit whose
intense gloom is unillumined even by the dim
light of the Davy lamp. Passages in even the
most mystical, so far as my reading of them

goes, however, are noted for real poetical beauty, and *Thel* is full of tenderness, sweetness, and delicacy throughout. Indeed, this is a real and genuine poem, and I say this without presuming to be able to decipher in clear terms the author's drift, for I do not regard that particular ability altogether essential before such a verdict is given, so long as the product possesses to me a meaning—an undefinable one though it may be—or constitutes spells by which visions of beauty and delight may be conjured up in my imagination, and visions of which the poet himself may never have dreamed—for it is in the nature of things that the seer may see further than he thinks; that the singer may sing more than he knows; that, in short, the poet's work may awaken and arouse the mind of the reader to the perception of a star-like galaxy of ideas, before whose dazzling splendour the light of his own particular drift may seem in comparison but the

insignificant piece of yellow flame of a farthing
candle. All of our very highest inspired work
is noted for this character, and Blake's best
is pre-eminently so ; while some of his most
imperfect has a touch of it. And as his work
was, so was the man. Lofty-minded, noble and
sweet in disposition and general temper, he yet
when crossed was subject to fits and outbursts
of anger and spleen, which, however, were only
for the moment, and the effects of which were
felt by none so keenly as by himself—which
were always followed by a spirit of child-like
forgetfulness or forgiveness, or in a spirit which
caused his irritability to be forgotten or for-
given, and which left the man the same object
of affection to his friends at the last that he
was to them at the first. Hence the secret of
the fact that though, from several causes anything but discreditable to himself, the circle of
his friends was small, these friends were, with
perhaps a single exception, life-friends ; and

when he had outlived nearly all these—for he did—he had the consolation to find himself begirt by a small knot of other—younger—ones more enthusiastic on the whole, and equally true—nearly all talented young artists, and who were not only destined to cheer him in his latter days, and soften with their sympathy the pillow of his death-bed, but to prove instrumental after his death in extending his fame and in defending his conduct and character, and who clearly held their friend and mentor to be wholly sane, whatever might from his words, deeds, or works be adduced by others as proofs to the contrary.

He died upon a Sunday, being the 12th of August 1827, in his seventieth year of age, and without issue, leaving his beloved wife Catherine, who outlived him four years, a sufficient capital in his works to supply her small wants. Setting aside the testimony of brother artists and other famous personages, it is proof sufficient that Blake had the purest and sweetest of dispositions to know that he was not only beloved by this excellent woman, but worshipped ; and as a small yet precious appendage to this grand testimony, I would add that a humble female who had sat with her by his death-bed, declared afterwards, "I have been at the death, not of a man, but of a blessed angel." That I conceive to be worth all the epitaphs to be found in all the church-yards and churches in Great Britain, with those in Westminster Abbey at their head.

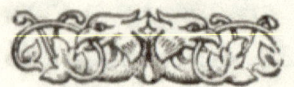

ADVERTISEMENT.

———◆———

THE following Sketches were the production of untutored youth, commenced in his twelfth, and occasionally resumed by the author till his twentieth year; since which time, his talents having been wholly directed to the attainment of excellence in his profession, he has been deprived of the leisure requisite to such a revisal of these sheets as might have rendered them less unfit to meet the public eye.

Conscious of the irregularities and defects to be found in almost every page, his friends have still believed that they possessed a poetical originality which merited some respite from oblivion. These their opinions remain, however, to be now reproved or confirmed by a less partial public.

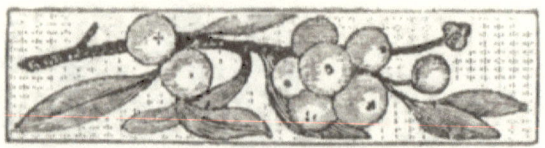

Poetical Sketches.

TO SPRING.

O THOU with dewy locks, who lookest down
  Through the clear windows of the morning,
    turn
Thine angel eyes upon our western isle,
Which in full choir hails thy approach, O Spring !

The hills tell each other, and the listening
Valleys hear ; all our longing eyes are turned
Up to thy bright pavilions : issue forth,
And let thy holy feet visit our clime !

Come o'er the eastern hills, and let our winds
Kiss thy perfumèd garments ; let us taste
Thy morn and evening breath ; scatter thy pearls
Upon our lovesick land that mourns for thee.

Oh, deck her forth with thy fair fingers ; pour
Thy soft kisses on her bosom ; and put
Thy golden crown upon her languished head,
Whose modest tresses were bound up for thee !

———

TO SUMMER.

O THOU who passest through our valleys in
  Thy strength, curb thy fierce steeds, allay
    the heat
That flames from their large nostrils ! Thou, O
    Summer,
Oft pitchedst here thy golden tent, and oft
Beneath our oaks has slept, while we beheld
With Joy thy ruddy limbs and flourishing hair.

Beneath our thickest shades we oft have heard
Thy voice, when Noon upon his fervid car
Rode o'er the deep of heaven. Beside our springs
Sit down, and in our mossy valleys, on
Some bank beside a river clear, throw thy

Silk draperies off, and rush into the stream !
Our valleys love the Summer in his pride.

Our bards are famed who strike the silver wire :
Our youth are bolder than the southern swains,
Our maidens fairer in the sprightly dance.
We lack not songs, nor instruments of joy,
Nor echoes sweet, nor waters clear as heaven,
Nor laurel wreaths against the sultry heat.

———

TO AUTUMN.

O AUTUMN, laden with fruit, and stained
  With the blood of the grape, pass not, but sit
Beneath my shady roof, there thou mayst rest,
And tune thy jolly voice to my fresh pipe,
And all the daughters of the year shall dance !
Sing now the lusty song of fruits and flowers.

" The narrow bud opens her beauties to
The sun, and love runs in her thrilling veins ;

Blossoms hang round the brows of Morning, and
Flourish down the bright cheek of modest Eve,
Till clustering summer breaks forth into singing,
And feathered clouds strew flowers round her head.

" The Spirits of the Air live on the smells
Of fruit ; and Joy, with pinions light, roves round
The gardens, or sits singing in the trees."
Thus sang the jolly Autumn as he sat ;
Then rose, girded himself, and o'er the bleak
Hills fled from our sight ; but left his golden load.

TO WINTER.

O WINTER ! bar thine adamantine doors :
    The north is thine ; there hast thou built thy
        dark
Deep-founded habitation.   Shake not thy roofs,
Nor bend thy pillars with thine iron car.

He hears me not, but o'er the yawning deep
Rides heavy ; his storms are unchained, sheathed
In ribbèd steel ; I dare not lift mine eyes ;
For he hath reared his sceptre o'er the world.

Lo ! now the direful monster, whose skin clings
To his strong bones, strides o'er the groaning
    rocks :
He withers all in silence, and in his hand
Unclothes the earth, and freezes up frail life.

He takes his seat upon the cliffs—the mariner
Cries in vain.　Poor little wretch, that deal'st
With storms !—till heaven smiles, and the monster
Is driven yelling to his caves beneath Mount
    Hecla.

TO THE EVENING STAR.

THOU fair-haired Angel of the Evening,
    Now, whilst the sun rests on the mountains,
       light
Thy bright torch of love—thy radiant crown
Put on, and smile upon our evening bed !
Smile on our loves ; and, while thou drawest the
Blue curtains of the sky, scatter thy silver dew
On every flower that shuts its sweet eyes
In timely sleep.   Let thy west wind sleep on
The lake ; speak silence with thy glimmering eyes,
And wash the dusk with silver.   Soon, full soon,
Dost thou withdraw ; then the wolf rages wide,
And the lion glares through the dun forest.
The fleeces of our flocks are covered with
Thy sacred dew : protect them with thine influence !

TO MORNING.

O HOLY virgin, clad in purest white,
  Unlock heaven's golden gates, and issue
    forth ;
Awake the dawn that sleeps in heaven ; let light
Rise from the chambers of the east, and bring
The honeyed dew that cometh on waking day.
O radiant Morning, salute the Sun,
Roused like a huntsman to the chase, and with
Thy buskined feet appear upon our hills.

FAIR ELEANOR.

THE bell struck one, and shook the silent tower ;
  The graves gave up their dead : fair Eleanor
Walked by the castle-gate, and lookèd in :
A hollow groan ran through the dreary vaults

She shrieked aloud, and sunk upon the steps,
On the cold stone her pale cheek. Sickly smells
Of death issue as from a sepulchre,
And all is silent but the sighing vaults.

Chill Death withdraws his hand, and she revives ;
Amazed she finds herself upon her feet,
And, like a ghost, through narrow passages
Walking, feeling the cold walls with her hands.

Fancy returns, and now she thinks of bones
And grinning skulls, and corruptible death
Wrapt in his shroud ; and now fancies she hears
Deep sighs, and sees pale sickly ghosts gliding.

At length, no fancy but reality
Distracts her.   A rushing sound, and the feet
Of one that fled, approaches.—Ellen stood,
Like a dumb statue, froze to stone with fear.

The wretch approaches, crying : "The deed is
    done !
Take this, and send it by whom thou wilt send ;
It is my life—send it to Eleanor :—
He's dead, and howling after me for blood !

" Take this," he cried ; and thrust into her arms
A wet napkin, wrapt about ; then rushed
Past, howling.   She received into her arms
Pale death, and followed on the wings of fear.

They passed swift through the outer gate ; the
    wretch,
Howling, leaped o'er the wall into the moat,
Stifling in mud.   Fair Ellen passed the bridge,
And heard a gloomy voice cry, " Is it done ? "

As the deer wounded, Ellen flew over
The pathless plain ; as the arrows that fly
By night, destruction flies, and strikes in darkness.
She fled from fear, till at her house arrived.

Her maids await her ; on her bed she falls,
That bed of joy where erst her lord hath pressed.
"Ah, woman's fear !" she cried, "ah, cursed duke !
Ah, my dear lord ! ah, wretched Eleanor !

" My lord was like a flower upon the brows
Of lusty May !   Ah, life as frail as flower !
O ghastly Death ! withdraw thy cruel hand !
Seek'st thou that flower to deck thy horrid temples ;

" My lord was like a star in highest heaven
Drawn down to earth by spells and wickedness ;
My lord was like the opening eyes of Day,
When western winds creep softly o'er the flowers

" But he is darkened ; like the summer's noon
Clouded ; fall'n like the stately tree, cut down ;
The breath of heaven dwelt among his leaves.
O Eleanor, weak woman, filled with woe ! "

Thus having spoke, she raisèd up her head,
And saw the bloody napkin by her side,
Which in her arms she brought ; and now, tenfold
More terrified, saw it unfold itself.

Her eyes were fixed ; the bloody cloth unfolds,
Disclosing to her sight the murdered head
Of her dear lord, all ghastly pale, clotted
With gory blood ; it groaned, and thus it spake :

" O Eleanor, behold thy husband's head,
Who, sleeping on the stones of yonder tower,
Was reft of life by the accursèd duke :
A hired villain turned my sleep to death.

" O Eleanor, beware the cursèd duke ;
Oh, give not him thy hand, now I am dead.
He seeks thy love ; who, coward, in the night,
Hired a villain to bereave my life."

She sat with dead cold limbs, stiffened to stone ,
She took the gory head up in her arms ;
She kissed the pale lips ; she had no tears to shed ;
She hugged it to her breast, and groaned her last.

D

SONG.

H OW sweet I roamed from field to field,
　　And tasted all the summer's pride,
Till I the Prince of Love beheld
　　Who in the sunny beams did glide.

He showed me lilies for my hair,
　　And blushing roses for my brow :
He led me through his gardens fair
　　Where all his golden pleasures grow.

With sweet May-dews my wings were wet,
　　And Phœbus fired my vocal rage ;
He caught me in his silken net,
　　And shut me in his golden cage.

He loves to sit and hear me sing,
　　Then laughing, sports and plays with me ;
Then stretches out my golden wing,
　　And mocks my loss of liberty.

SONG.

MY silks and fine array,
　　My smiles and languished air,
By love are driven away ;
　And mournful lean Despair
Brings me yew to deck my grave :
Such end true lovers have.

His face is fair as heaven
　When springing buds unfold ;
Oh, why to him was't given,
　Whose heart is wintry cold?
His breast is love's all-worshipped tomb,
Where all love's pilgrims come.

Bring me an axe and spade,
　Bring me a winding-sheet ;
When I my grave have made,
　Let winds and tempests beat :
Then down I'll lie, as cold as clay.
True love doth pass away !

SONG.

L OVE and harmony combine,
        And around our souls entwine,
While thy branches mix with mine,
And our roots together join.

Joys upon our branches sit,
Chirping loud and singing sweet ;
Like gentle streams beneath our feet,
Innocence and virtue meet.

Thou the golden fruit dost bear,
I am clad in flowers fair ;
Thy sweet boughs perfume the air,
And the turtle buildeth there.

There she sits and feeds her young,
Sweet I hear her mournful song ;
And thy lovely leaves among
There is Love ; I hear his tongue.

There his charming nest doth lay,
There he sleeps the night away ;
There he sports along the day,
And doth among our branches play.

SONG.

I LOVE the jocund dance,
  The softly-breathing song,
Where innocent eyes do glance,
  And where lisps the maiden's tongue.

I love the laughing vale,
  I love the echoing hill,
Where mirth does never fail,
  And the jolly swain laughs his fill.

I love the pleasant cot,
  I love the innocent bower,
Where white and brown is our lot,
  Or fruit in the mid-day hour.

I love the oaken seat
   Beneath the oaken tree,
Where all the old villagers meet,
   And laugh our sports to see.

I love our neighbours all—
   But, Kitty, I better love thee ;
And love them I ever shall,
   But thou art all to me.

SONG.

MEMORY, hither come,
     And tune your merry notes :
And, while upon the wind
   Your music floats,
I'll pore upon the stream
Where sighing lovers dream,
And fish for fancies as they pass
Within the watery glass.

I'll drink of the clear stream,
   And hear the linnet's song,
And there I'll lie and dream
   The day along :
And, when night comes, I'll go
To places fit for woe,
Walking along the darkened valley
With silent Melancholy.

MAD SONG.

THE wild winds weep,
  And the night is a-cold ;
Come hither, Sleep,
  And my griefs enfold ! . . .
But lo ! the morning peeps
Over the eastern steeps,
And the rustling beds* of dawn
The earth do scorn.

Lo ! to the vault
  Of pavèd heaven,
With sorrow fraught,
  My notes are driven :
They strike the ear of Night,
  Make weep the eyes of Day ;
They make mad the roaring winds,
  And with tempests play.

Like a fiend in a cloud,
  With howling woe

* Evidently "birds," as in Gilchrist's edition.

After night I do crowd
   And with night will go ;
I turn my back to the east
From whence comforts have increased ;
For light doth seize my brain
With frantic pain.

SONG.

FRESH from the dewy hill the merry Year
   Smiles on my head, and mounts his flaming
      car ;
Round my young brows the laurel wreathes a
   shade,
And rising glories beam around my head.

My feet are winged, while o'er the dewy lawn
I meet my maiden risen like the morn.
Oh, bless those holy feet, like angels' feet ;
Oh, bless those limbs, beaming with heavenly
   light !

Like as an angel glittering in the sky
In times of innocence and holy joy ;
The joyful shepherd stops his grateful song
To hear the music of an angel's tongue.

So, when she speaks, the voice of Heaven I hear ;
So, when we walk, nothing impure comes near ;
Each field seems Eden, and each calm retreat ;
Each village seems the haunt of holy feet.

But that sweet village, where my black-eyed maid
Closes her eyes in sleep beneath night's shade,
Whene'er I enter, more than mortal fire
Burns in my soul, and does my song inspire.

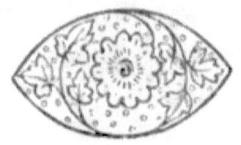

SONG.

WHEN early Morn walks forth in sober grey,
  Then to my black-eyed maid I haste away·
When Evening sits beneath her dusky bower,
And gently sighs away the silent hour,
The village bell alarms, away I go,
And the vale darkens at my pensive woe.

To that sweet village where my black-eyed maid
Doth drop a tear beneath the silent shade
I turn my eyes ; and pensive as I go,
Curse my black stars, and bless my pleasing woe.

Oft, when the Summer sleeps among the trees,
Whispering faint murmurs to the scanty breeze,
I walk the village round ; if at her side
A youth doth walk in stolen joy and pride,
I curse my stars in bitter grief and woe,
That made my love so high, and me so low.

Oh, should she e'er prove false, his limbs I'd tear
And throw all pity on the burning air !
I'd curse bright fortune for my mixèd lot,
And then I'd die in peace, and be forgot.

TO THE MUSES.

WHETHER on Ida's shady brow,
Or in the chambers of the East,
The chambers of the Sun, that now
From ancient melody have ceased ;

Whether in heaven ye wander fair,
Or the green corners of the earth,
Or the blue regions of the air
Where the melodious winds have birth ;

Whether on crystal rocks ye rove,
Beneath the bosom of the sea,
Wandering in many a coral grove ;
Fair Nine, forsaking Poetry ;

How have you left the ancient love
That bards of old enjoyed in you !
The languid strings do scarcely move,
The sound is forced, the notes are few !

GWIN, KING OF NORWAY.

COME, kings, and listen to my song.—
 When Gwin, the son of Nore,
Over the nations of the North
 His cruel sceptre bore ;

The nobles of the land did feed
 Upon the hungry poor ;
They tear the poor man's lamb, and drive
 The needy from their door.

" The land is desolate ! our wives
 And children cry for bread ;
Arise and pull the tyrant down !
 Let Gwin be humblèd ! "

Gordred the giant roused himself
 From sleeping in his cave ;
He shook the hills, and in the clouds
 The troubled banners wave.

Beneath them rolled, like tempests black,
  The numerous sons of blood ;
Like lions' whelps, roaring abroad,
  Seeking their nightly food.

Down Bleron's hills they dreadful rush,
  Their cry ascends the clouds ;
The trampling horse and clanging arms
  Like rushing mighty floods !

Their wives and children, weeping loud,
  Follow in wild array,
Howling like ghosts, furious as wolves
  In the bleak wintry day.

" Pull down the tyrant to the dust,
  Let Gwin be humbled,"
They cry, "and let ten thousand lives !
  Pay for the tyrant's head ! "

From tower to tower the watchmen cry :
  " O Gwin, the son of Nore,
Arouse thyself ! the nations, black
  Like clouds, came rolling o'er ! "

Gwin reared his shield, his palace shakes,
  His chiefs come rushing round ;
Each like an awful thunder-cloud
  With voice of solemn sound :

Like rearèd stones around a grave
  They stand around the king ;
Then suddenly each seized his spear,
  And clashing steel does ring.

The husbandman does leave his plough
  To wade through fields of gore ;
The merchant binds his brows in steel,
  And leaves the trading shore ;

The shepherd leaves his mellow pipe,
  And sounds the trumpet shrill ;
The workman throws his hammer down
  To heave the bloody bill.

Like the tall ghost of Barraton
  Who sports in stormy sky,
Gwin leads his host as black as night
  When pestilence does fly,

With horses and with chariots—
   And all his spearmen bold
March to the sound of mournful song,
   Like clouds around him rolled.

Gwin lifts his hand—the nations halt ;
   " Prepare for war ! " he cries.
Gordred appears !—his frowning brow
   Troubles our northern skies.

The armies stand, like balances
   Held in the Almighty's hand—
" Gwin, thou hast filled thy measure up :
   Thou'rt swept from out the land."

And now the raging armies rushed
   Like warring mighty seas ;
The heavens are shook with roaring war,
   The dust ascends the skies !

Earth smokes with blood, and groans and shakes
   To drink her children's gore,
A sea of blood ; nor can the eye
   See to the trembling shore.

And on the verge of this wild sea
    Famine and death do cry ;
The cries of women and of babes
    Over the field do fly.

The king is seen raging afar,
    With all his men of might ;
Like blazing comets scattering death
    Through the red feverous night.

Beneath his arm like sheep they die,
    And groan upon the plain ;
The battle faints, and bloody men
    Fight upon hills of slain.

Now death is sick, and riven men
    Labour and toil for life ;
Steed rolls on steed, and shield on shield,
    Sunk in this sea of strife !

The god of War is drunk with blood,
    The earth doth faint and fail ;
The stench of blood makes sick the heavens
    Ghosts glut the throat of hell !

E

Oh, what have kings to answer for
　　Before that awful throne,
When thousand deaths for vengeance cry,
　　And ghosts accusing groan !

Like blazing comets in the sky
　　That shake the stars of light,
Which drop like fruit unto the earth
　　Through the fierce burning night ;

Like these did Gwin and Gordred meet,
　　And the first blow decides ;
Down from the brow unto the breast
　　Gordred his head divides !

Gwin fell : the Sons of Norway fled,
　　All that remained alive ;
The rest did fill the vale of death—
　　For them the eagles strive.

The river Dorman rolled their blood
　　Into the northern sea ;
Who mourned his sons, and overwhelmed
　　The pleasant south country.

AN IMITATION OF SPENSER.

GOLDEN Apollo, that through heaven wide
  Scatter'st the rays of light, and truth his
   beams,
In lucent words my darkling voices dight,
 And wash my earthly mind in thy clear streams,
 That wisdom may descend in fairy dreams,
All while the jocund Hours in thy train
 Scatter their fancies at thy poet's feet ;
And, when thou yield'st to Night thy wide domain,
 Let rays of truth enlight his sleeping brain.

For brutish Pan in vain might thee assay
 With tinkling sounds to dash thy nervous verse,
Sound without sense ; yet in his rude affray
 (For Ignorance is folly's leasing nurse,
 And love of Folly needs none other's curse)
Midas the praise hath gained of lengthened ears,
 For which himself might deem him ne'er the
   worse
To sit in council with his modern peers,
 And judge of tinkling rhymes and elegances terse.

And thou, Mercurius, that with wingèd bow
   Dost mount aloft into the yielding sky,
And through heaven's halls thy airy flight dost
      throw,
   Entering with holy feet to where on high
   Jove weighs the counsel of futurity ;
Then laden with eternal fate, dost go
   Down, like a fallen star, from Autumn sky,
   And o'er the surface of the silent deep dost fly :

If thou arrivest at the sandy shore
   Where nought but envious hissing adders dwell,
Thy golden rod thrown on the dusty floor,
   Can charm to harmony with potent spell ;
   Such is sweet Eloquence, that does dispel
Envy and Hate that thirst for human gore ;
   And cause in sweet society to dwell
   Vile savage minds that lurk in lonely cell.

O Mercury, assist my labouring sense
   That round the circle of the world would fly,
As the winged eagle scorns the towery fence
    Of Alpine hills round his high aëry,

And searches through the corners of the sky,
Sports in the clouds to hear the thunder's sound,
   And see the winged lightnings as they fly ;
Then, bosomed in an amber cloud, around
   Plumes his wide wings, and seeks Sol's palace
     high.

And thou, O warrior maid invincible,
   Armed with the terrors of Almighty Jove,
Pallas, Minerva, maiden terrible,
   Lov'st thou to walk the peaceful solemn grove,
   In solemn gloom of branches interwove ?

   Or bear'st thy ægis o'er the burning field
     Where like the sea the waves of battle move ?
   Or have thy soft piteous eyes beheld
     The weary wanderer through the desert rove ?
Or does the afflicted man thy heavenly bosom
     move ?

BLIND-MAN'S BUFF.

WHEN silver snow decks Susan's clothes,
　　And jewels hang at th' shepherd's nose,
The blushing bank is all my care,
With hearth so red, and walls so fair.
" Heap the sea-coal, come, heap it higher ;
The oaken log lay on the fire."
The well-washed stools, a circling row,
With lad and lass, how fair the show !
The merry can of nut-brown ale,
The laughing jest, the love-sick tale—
Till, tired of chat, the game begins.
The lasses prick the lads with pins.
Roger from Dolly twitched the stool ;
She, falling, kissed the ground, poor fool !
She blushed so red, with sidelong glance
At hobnail Dick, who grieved the chance.
But now for Blind-man's Buff they call ;
Of each incumbrance clear the hall.

Jenny her silken kerchief folds,
And blear-eyed Will the black lot holds.

Now laughing stops, with " Silence, hush ! "
And Peggy Pout gives Sam a push.
The blind-man's arms, extended wide,
Sam slips between :—" Oh, woe betide
Thee, clumsy Will ! "—but tittering Kate
Is penned up in the corner strait !
And now Will's eyes beheld the play ;
He thought his face was t'other way.
" Now, Kitty, now ! what chance hast thou ?
Roger so near thee trips, I vow ! "
She catches him—then Roger ties
His own head up—but not his eyes ;
For through the slender cloth he sees,
And runs at Sam, who slips with ease
His clumsy hold ; and, dodging round,
Sukey is tumbled on the ground.
" See what it is to play unfair !
Where cheating is, there's mischief there."
But Roger still pursues the chase,
" He sees ! he sees ! " cries softly Grace ;
" O Roger, thou, unskilled in art,
Must, surer bound, go through thy part ! "

Now Kitty, pert, repeats the rhymes,
And Roger turns him round three times,
Then pauses ere he starts.   But Dick
Was mischief-bent upon a trick ;
Down on his hands and knees he lay
Directly in the Blind-man's way,   [ran,
Then cries out " Hem ! "—Hodge heard, and
With hood-winked chance—sure of his man ;
But down he came.—Alas, how frail
Our best of hopes, how soon they fail !
With crimson drops he stains the ground ;
Confusion startles all around.
Poor piteous Dick supports his head,
And fain would cure the hurt he made.
But Kitty hasted with a key,
And down his back they straight convey
The cold relief : the blood is stayed,
And Hodge again holds up his head.

Such are the fortunes of the game ;
And those who play should stop the same
By wholesome laws. such as—All those
Who on the blinded man impose

Stand in his stead ; as, long agone,
When men were first a nation grown,
Lawless they lived, till wantonness
And liberty began to increase,
And one man lay in another's way ;
Then laws were made to keep fair play.

A WAR SONG:

TO ENGLISHMEN.

PREPARE, prepare the iron helm of war,
    Bring forth the lots, cast in the spacious orb ;
The Angel of Fate turns them with mighty hands,
And casts them out upon the darkened earth !
              Prepare, prepare !

Prepare your hearts for Death's cold hand ! prepare
Your souls for flight, your bodies for the earth !
Prepare your arms for glorious victory !
Prepare your eyes to meet a holy God !
              Prepare, prepare !

Whose fatal scroll is that ?   Methinks 'tis mine !
Why sinks my heart, why faltereth my tongue ?
Had I three lives, I'd die in such a cause,
And rise, with ghosts, over the well-fought field.
                    Prepare, prepare !

The arrows of Almighty God are drawn !
Angels of Death stand in the low'ring heavens !
Thousands of souls must seek the realms of light,
And walk together on the clouds of heaven !
                    Prepare, prepare !

Soldiers, prepare !   Our cause is Heaven's cause ;
Soldiers, prepare !   Be worthy of our cause :
Prepare to meet our fathers in the sky :
Prepare, O troops that are to fall to-day !
                    Prepare, prepare !

Alfred shall smile, and make his heart rejoice ;
The Norman William and the learned Clerk,
And Lion-Heart, and black-browed Edward with
His loyal queen, shall rise, and welcome us !
                    Prepare, prepare !

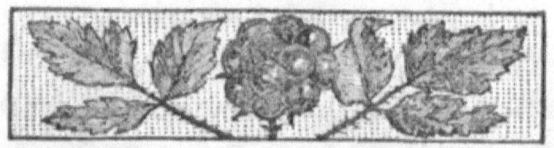

SAMSON.

SAMSON, the strongest of the children of men,
I sing ; how he was foiled by woman's arts,
By a false wife brought to the gates of death.
O Truth, that shinest with propitious beams,
Turning our earthly night to heavenly day,
From presence of the Almighty Father thou
Visitest our darkling world with blessed feet,
Bringing good news of Sin and Death destroyed !
O white-robed Angel, guide my timorous hand
To write as on a lofty rock with iron pen
The words of truth, that all who pass may read.

Now Night, noon-tide of damnèd spirits,
Over the silent earth spreads her pavilion,
While in dark council sat Philistia's lords ;
And, where strength failed, black thoughts in
    ambush lay.

There helmèd youth and aged warriors
In dust together lie, and Desolation
Spreads his wings over the land of Palestine :
From side to side the land groans, her prowess lost,
And seeks to hide her bruisèd head
Under the mists of night, breeding dark plots.
For Dalila's fair arts have long been tried in vain ;
In vain she wept in many a treacherous tear.
Go on, fair traitress ; do thy guileful work !
Ere once again the changing moon
Her circuit hath performed, thou shalt overcome,
And conquer him by force unconquerable,
And wrest his secret from him.
Call thine alluring arts and honest-seeming brow,
The holy kiss of love and the transparent tear ;
Put on fair linen that with the lily vies,
Purple and silver ; neglect thy hair, to seem
More lovely in thy loose attire ; put on
Thy country's pride, deceit, and eyes of love
Decked in mild sorrow ; and sell thy lord for gold.

For now, upon her sumptuous couch reclined
In gorgeous pride, she still entreats, and still

She grasps his vigorous knees with her fair arms.
"Thou lov'st me not ! thou'rt war, thou art not
　　love !
O foolish Dalila !　O weak woman !
It is Death clothed in flesh thou lovest,
And thou hast been encircled in his arms !
Alas, my lord, what am I calling thee ?
Thou art my God !　To thee I pour my tears
For sacrifice morning and evening :
My days are covered with sorrow ; shut up,
　　darkened :
By night I am deceived !
Who says that thou wast born of mortal kind ?
Destruction was thy father, a lioness
Suckled thee, thy young hands tore human limbs,
And gorgèd human flesh !
Come hither, Death ; art thou not Samson's
　　servant ?
'Tis Dalila that calls—thy master's wife.
No, stay, and let thy master do the deed :
One blow of that strong arm would ease my
　　pain ;
Then I should lie at quiet and have rest.

Pity forsook thee at thy birth !   O Dagon
Furious, and all ye gods of Palestine,
Withdraw your hand !   I am but a weak woman.
Alas, I am wedded to your enemy !
I will go mad, and tear my crisped hair ;
I'll run about, and pierce the ears o' the gods !
O Samson, hold me not ; thou lov'st me not !
Look not upon me with those deathful eyes !
Thou wouldst my death, and death, approaches
    fast."
Thus, in false tears, she bathed his feet,
And thus she day by day oppressed his soul.
He seemed a mountain, his brow among the clouds ;
She seemed a silver stream, his feet embracing.

Dark thoughts rolled to and fro in his mind,
Like thunder-clouds troubling the sky ;
His visage was troubled ; his soul was distressed.
"Though I should tell her all my heart, what can
    I fear ?
Though I should tell this secret of my birth,
The utmost may be warded off as well when told as
    now."

She saw him moved, and thus resumes her wiles,
"Samson, I am thine ; do with me what thou wilt ;
My friends are enemies ; my life is death ;
I am a traitor to my nation, and despised ;
My joy is given into the hands of him
Who hates me, using deceit to the wife of his
  bosom.
Thrice hast thou mocked me and grieved my
  soul.
Didst thou not tell me with green withes to bind
Thy nervous arms, and, after that,
When I had found thy falsehood, with new ropes
To bind thee fast ? I knew thou didst but mock
  me.
Alas, when in thy sleep I bound thee with them,
To try thy truth, I cried, ' The Philistines
Be upon thee, Samson !' Then did suspicion wake
  thee ;
How didst thou rend the feeble ties !
Thou fearest nought, what shouldst thou fear ?
Thy power is more than mortal, none can hurt
  thee ;
Thy bones are brass, thy sinews are iron ;

Ten thousand spears are like the summer grass ;
An army of mighty men are as flocks in the
   valleys :
What canst thou fear ? I drink my tears like
   water :
I live upon sorrow ! O worse than wolves and
   tigers,
What canst thou give when such a trifle is denied
   me ?
But oh ! at last thou mockest me, to shame
My over-fond inquiry !   Thou told'st me
To weave thee to the beam by thy strong hair ;
I did even that to try thy truth ; but, when
I cried, 'The Philistines be upon thee !' then
Didst thou leave me to bewail that Samson loved
   me not."

He sat, and inward grieved :
He saw and loved the beauteous suppliant,
Nor could conceal aught that might appease her.
Then, leaning on her bosom, thus he spoke :
" Hear, O Dalila ! doubt no more of Samson's
   love ;

For that fair breast was made the ivory palace
Of my inmost heart, where it shall lie at rest.
For sorrow is the lot of all of woman born :
For care was I brought forth, and labour is my lot :
Nor matchless might, nor wisdom, nor every gift
    enjoyed,
Can from the heart of man hide sorrow.
Twice was my birth foretold from heaven, and
    twice
A sacred vow enjoined me that I should drink
No wine, nor eat of any unclean thing,
For holy unto Israel's God I am,
A Nazarite even from my mother's womb.
Twice was it told, that it might not be broken.
'Grant me a son, kind Heaven,' Manoa cried ;
But Heaven refused.
Childless he mourned, but thought his God knew
    best.
In solitude, though not obscure, in Israel
He lived, till venerable age came on :
His flocks increased, and plenty crowned his
    board :
Beloved, revered of man.   But God hath other joys
     F

In store.   Is burdened Israel his grief?
The son of his old age shall set it free !
The venerable sweetener of his life
Receives the promise first from heaven.   She saw
The maidens play, and blessed their innocent mirth ;
She blessed each new-joined pair ; but from her
The long-wished deliverer shall spring.
Pensive, alone she sat within the house,
When busy day was fading, and calm evening,
Time for contemplation, rose
From the forsaken east, and drew the curtains of
     heaven.
Pensive she sat, and thought on Israel's grief,
And silent prayed to Israel's God ; when lo !
An angel from the fields of light entered the house.
His form was manhood in the prime,
And from his spacious brow shot terrors through
     the evening shade.
But mild he hailed her—' Hail, highly favoured ! '
     said he ;
' For lo ! thou shalt conceive, and bear a son,
And Israel's strength shall be upon his shoulders,
And he shall be called Israel's Deliverer.

Now, therefore, drink no wine, and eat not any
    unclean thing,
For he shall be a Nazarite to God.'
Then, as a neighbour, when his evening tale is told,
Departs, his blessing leaving, so seemed he to depart :
She wondered with exceeding joy, nor knew he
    was an angel.
Manoa left his fields to sit in the house,
And take his evening's rest from labour—
The sweetest time that God has allotted mortal
    man.
He sat, and heard with joy,
And praisèd God, who Israel still doth keep.
The time rolled on, and Israel groaned oppressed.
The sword was bright, while the ploughshare rusted,
Till hope grew feeble, and was ready to give place
    to doubting.
Then prayed Manoa :
'O Lord, thy flock is scattered on the hills—
The wolf teareth them ;
Oppression stretches his rod over our land ;
Our country is ploughed with swords, and reaped
    in blood ;

The echoes of slaughter reach from hill to hill ;
Instead of peaceful pipe the shepherd bears
A sword ; the ox-goad is turned into a spear !
Oh, when shall our Deliverer come ?
The Philistine riots on our flocks,
Our vintage is gathered by bands of enemies !
Stretch forth thy hand and save.'—Thus prayed
    Manoa.
The aged woman walked into the field,
And lo ! again the angel came,
Clad as a traveller fresh risen on his journey.
She ran and called her husband, who came and
    talked with him.
' O man of God,' said he, 'thou com'st from far !
Let us detain thee while I make ready a kid,
That thou mayst sit and eat, and tell us of thy
    name and warfare ;
That, when thy sayings come to pass, we may
    honour thee.'
The angel answered, ' My name is Wonderful ;
Inquire not after it, seeing it is a secret ;
But if thou wilt, offer an offering unto the Lord.'"

KING EDWARD THE THIRD.

PERSONS.

KING EDWARD.   SIR THOMAS DAGWORTH.
THE BLACK PRINCE.   SIR WALTER MANNY.
QUEEN PHILIPPA.   LORD AUDLEY.
DUKE OF CLARENCE.   LORD PERCY.
SIR JOHN CHANDOS.   BISHOP.
WILLIAM, *Dagworth's man.*
PETER BLUNT, *a common soldier.*

SCENE.—*The Coast of France.*

KING EDWARD *and Nobles before it.* *The Army.*

KING

O THOU, to whose fury the nations are
     But as dust ! maintain thy servant's right.
Without thine aid, the twisted mail, and spear,
And forgèd helm, and shield of seven-times beaten
     brass

Are idle trophies of the vanquisher.
When confusion rages, when the field is in a flame,
When the cries of blood tear horror from heaven,
And yelling Death runs up and down the ranks,
Let Liberty, the chartered right of Englishmen,
Won by our fathers in many a glorious field,
Enerve my soldiers ; let Liberty
Blaze in each countenance, and fire the battle.
The enemy fight in chains, invisible chains, but
    heavy ;
Their minds are fettered ; then how can they be
    free ?
While, like the mounting flame,
We spring to battle o'er the floods of death !
And these fair youths, the flower of England,
Venturing their lives in my most righteous cause,
Oh, sheathe their hearts with triple steel, that they
May emulate their fathers' virtues !
And thou, my son, be strong ; thou fightest for a
    crown
That death can never ravish from thy brow—
A crown of glory—but from thy very dust
Shall beam a radiance, to fire the breasts

Of youth unborn !   Our names are written equal
In Fame's wide-trophied hall ; 'tis ours to gild
The letters, and to make them shine with gold
That never tarnishes : whether Third Edward,
Or the Prince of Wales, or Montacute, or Mortimer,
Or ev'n the least by birth, shall gain the brightest
        fame,
Is in His hand to whom all men are equal.
The world of men are like the numerous stars
That beam and twinkle in the depth of night,
Each clad in glory according to his sphere ;
But we, that wander from our native seats
And beam forth lustre on a darkling world,
Grow large as we advance : and some, perhaps,
The most obscure at home, that scarce were seen
To twinkle in their sphere, may so advance
That the astonished world, with upturned eyes,
Regardless of the moon, and those that once were
        bright,
Stand only for to gaze upon their splendour.
        [*He here knights the Prince and other
                young nobles.*
Now let us take a just revenge for those

Brave Lords who fell beneath the bloody axe
At Paris.   Thanks, noble Harcourt, for 'twas
By your advice we landed here in Brittany,
A country not yet sown with destruction,
And where the fiery whirlwind of swift war
Has not yet swept its desolating wing.
Into three parties we divide by day,
And separate march, but join again at night :
Each knows his rank, and heaven marshal all.

                              [*Exeunt.*

SCENE.—*English Court.*

LIONEL, DUKE OF CLARENCE, QUEEN PHILIPPA,
Lords, Bishops, etc.

CLARENCE.

My Lords, I have by the advice of her
Whom I am doubly bound to obey, my parent
And my sovereign, called you together.
My task is great, my burden heavier than
My unfledged years ;

Yet with your kind assistance, Lords, I hope
England shall dwell in peace : that, while my
    father
Toils in his wars, and turns his eyes on this
His native shore, and sees commerce fly round
With his white wings, and sees his golden London
And her silver Thames thronged with shining
    spires
And corded ships, her merchants buzzing round
Like summer bees, and all the golden cities
In his land overflowing with honey,
Glory may not be dimmed with clouds of care.
Say, Lords, should not our thoughts be first to
    commerce ?
My Lord Bishop, you would recommend us agri-
    culture ?

BISHOP.

Sweet Prince, the arts of peace are great,
And no less glorious than those of war,
Perhaps more glorious in the philosophic mind.
When I sit at my home, a private man,
My thoughts are on my gardens and my fields,

How to employ the hand that lacketh bread.
If Industry is in my diocese,
Religion will flourish ; each man's heart
Is cultivated, and will bring forth fruit :
This is my private duty and my pleasure.
But, as I sit in council with my prince,
My thoughts take in the general good of the whole,
And England is the land favoured by commerce ;
For Commerce, though the child of Agriculture,
Fosters his parent, who else must sweat and toil,
And gain but scanty fare.   Then my dear Lord,
Be England's trade our care ; and we as trades-
    men
Looking to the gain of this our native land.

CLARENCE.

O my good Lord, true wisdom drops like honey
From your tongue, as from a worshipped oak !
Forgive, my Lords, my talkative youth, that speaks
Not merely what my narrow observation has
Picked up, but what I have concluded from your
    lessons.

Now, by the Queen's advice, I ask your leave
To dine to-morrow with the Mayor of London :
If I obtain your leave, I have another boon
To ask, which is the favour of your company.
I fear Lord Percy will not give me leave.

PERCY.

Dear Sir, a prince should always keep his state,
And grant his favours with a sparing hand,
Or they are never rightly valued.
These are my thoughts : yet it were best to go :
But keep a proper dignity, for now
You represent the sacred person of
Your father ; 'tis with princes as 'tis with the sun ;
If not sometimes o'erclouded, we grow weary
Of his officious glory.

CLARENCE.

Then you will give me leave to shine sometimes,
My Lord?

LORD (*aside*).

Thou has a gallant spirit which I fear
Will be imposed on by the closer sort.

CLARENCE.

Well, I'll endeavour to take
Lord Percy's advice ; I have been used so much
To dignity that I'm sick on't.

QUEEN PHILIPPA.

Fie, fie, Lord Clarence ! you proceed not to
    business,
But speak of your own pleasures.
I hope their lordships will excuse your giddiness.

CLARENCE

My Lords, the French have fitted out many
Small ships of war that, like to raving wolves,
Infest our English seas, devouring all
Our burdened vessels, spoiling our naval flocks.
The merchants do complain, and beg our aid.

PERCY.

The merchants are rich enough ;
Can they not help themselves?

BISHOP.

They can, and may ; but how to gain their will
Requires our countenance and help.

PERCY.

When that they find they must, my Lord, they will
Let them but suffer awhile, and you shall see
They will bestir themselves.

BISHOP.

Lord Percy cannot mean that we should suffer
This disgrace.   If so, we are not sovereigns
Of the sea—our right, that heaven gave
To England, when at the birth of Nature
She was seated in the deep ; the Ocean ceased
His mighty roar, and, fawning, played around
Her snowy feet, and owned his awful Queen.
Lord Percy, if the heart is sick, the head
Must be aggrieved ; if but one member suffer,
The heart doth fail.   You say, my Lord, the
        merchants
Can, if they will, defend themselves against

These rovers : this is a noble scheme,
Worthy the brave Lord Percy, and as worthy
His generous aid to put it into practice.

PERCY.

Lord Bishop, what was rash in me is wise
In you ; I dare not own the plan.   'Tis not
Mine.   Yet will I, if you please,
Quickly to the Lord Mayor, and work him onward
To this most glorious voyage ; on which cast
I'll set my whole estate,
But we will bring these Gallic rovers under.

QUEEN PHILIPPA.

Thanks, brave Lord Percy ; you have the thanks
Of England's Queen, and will, ere long, of England.

       [Exeunt.

SCENE.—*At Cressy.*

SIR THOMAS DAGWORTH *and* LORD AUDLEY
meeting.

AUDLEY.

Good-morrow, brave Sir Thomas ; the bright morn
Smiles on our army, and the gallant sun
Springs from the hills like a young hero
Into the battle, shaking his golden locks
Exultingly : this is a promising day.

DAGWORTH.

Why, my Lord Audley, I don't know.
Give me your hand, and now I'll tell you what
I think you do not know.   Edward's afraid of
　　Philip.

AUDLEY.

Ha, ha ! Sir Thomas ! you but joke ;
Did you e'er see him fear ?   At Blanchetaque,
When almost singly he drove six thousand
French from the ford, did he fear then ?

DAGWORTH.

Yes, fear—that made him fight so.

AUDLEY.

By the same reason I might say 'tis fear
That makes you fight.

DAGWORTH.

Mayhap you may.　Look upon Edward's face,
No one can say he fears ; but, when he turns
His back, then I will say it to his face ;　.
He is afraid : he makes us all afraid.
I cannot bear the enemy at my back.
Now here we are at Cressy ; where to-morrow,
To-morrow we shall know.　I say, Lord Audley
That Edward runs away from Philip.

AUDLEY.

Perhaps you think the Prince, too, is afraid ?

DAGWORTH.

No : God forbid ! I'm sure he is **not.**

He is a young lion.   Oh, I have seen him fight
And give command, and lightning has flashed
From his eyes across the field : I have seen him
Shake hands with Death, and strike a bargain for
The enemy ; he has danced in the field
Of battle, like the youth at morris-play.
I'm sure he's not afraid, nor Warwick, nor none,
None of us but me, and I am very much afraid.

AUDLEY.

Are you afraid, too, Sir Thomas ?
I believe that as much as I believe
The King's afraid : but what are you afraid of ?

DAGWORTH.

Of having my back laid open ; we turn
Our backs to the fire, till we shall burn our skirts.

AUDLEY.

And this, Sir Thomas, you call fear ?   Your fear
Is of a different kind, then, from the King's ;

G

He fears to turn his face, and you to turn your
    back.
I do not think, Sir Thomas, you know what fear is

Enter SIR JOHN CHANDOS.

CHANDOS.

Good-morrow, Generals ; I give you joy :
Welcome to the fields of Cressy.   Here we stop,
And wait for Philip.

DAGWORTH.

I hope so

AUDLEY.

There, Sir Thomas ; do you call that fear ?

DAGWORTH.

I don't know ; perhaps he takes it by fits.
Why, noble Chandos, look you here—
One rotten sheep spoils the whole flock ;
And if the bell-wether is tainted, I wish
The Prince may not catch the distemper too.

CHANDOS.

Distemper, Sir Thomas ! what distemper ?
I have not heard.

DAGWORTH.

Why, Chandos, you are a wise man,
I know you understand me ; a distemper
The King caught here in France of running away.

AUDLEY.

Sir Thomas, you say you have caught it too.

DAGWORTH.

And so will the whole army ; 'tis very catching,
For, when the coward runs, the brave man totters.
Perhaps the air of the country is the cause.
I feel it coming upon me, so I strive against it ;
You yet are whole ; but, after a few more
Retreats, we all shall know how to retreat
Better than fight.—To be plain, I think retreating
Too often takes away a soldier's courage.

CHANDOS.

Here comes the King himself : tell him your
    thoughts
Plainly, Sir Thomas.

DAGWORTH.

I've told him before, but his disorder
Makes him deaf.

Enter KING EDWARD *and* BLACK PRINCE.

KING.

Good-morrow, Generals ; when English courage
    fails,
Down goes our right to France.
But we are conquerers everywhere ; nothing
Can stand our soldiers ; each man is worthy
Of a triumph.   Such an army of heroes
Ne'er shouted to the heavens, nor shook the field.
Edward, my son, thou art
Most happy, having such command : the man
Were base who were not fired to deeds
Above heroic, having such examples.

PRINCE.

Sire, with respect and deference I look
Upon such noble souls, and wish myself
Worthy the high command that Heaven and you
Have given me.   When I have seen the field glow,
And in each countenance the soul of war
Curbed by the manliest reason, I have been winged
With certain victory ; and 'tis my boast,
And shall be still my glory, I was inspired
By these brave troops.

DAGWORTH.

Your Grace had better make them
All Generals.

KING.

Sir Thomas Dagworth, you must have your joke,
And shall, while you can fight as you did at
The Ford.

DAGWORTH.

I have a small petition to your Majesty.

KING.

What can Sir Thomas Dagworth ask
That Edward can refuse ?

DAGWORTH.

I hope your Majesty cannot refuse so great
A trifle ; I've gilt your cause with my best blood,
And would again, were I not forbid
By him whom I am bound to obey: my hands
Are tied up, my courage shrunk and withered,
My sinews slackened, and my voice scarce heard ;
Therefore I beg I may return to England.

KING.

I know not what you could have asked, Sir
    Thomas,
That I would not have sooner parted with
Than such a soldier as you have been, and such a
    friend :
Nay, I will know the most remote particulars
Of this your strange petition ; that, if I can
I still may keep you here.

DAGWORTH.

Here on the fields of Cressy we are settled
Till Philip springs the timorous covey again.
The wolf is hunted down by causeless fear ;
The lion flees, and fear usurps his heart,
Startled, astonished at the clamorous cock ;
The eagle, that doth gaze upon the sun,
Fears the small fire that plays about the fen.
If at this moment of their idle fear
The dog doth seize the wolf, the forester the lion,
The negro in the crevice of the rock
Doth seize the soaring eagle ; undone by flight,
They tame submit : such the effect flight has
On noble souls.   Now hear its opposite :
The timorous stag starts from the thicket wild,
The fearful crane springs from the splashy fen,
The shining snake glides o'er the bending grass,
The stag turns head, and bays the crying hounds ;
The crane o'ertaken fighteth with the hawk ;
The snake doth turn, and bite the padding foot.
And if your Majesty's afraid of Philip,
You are more like a lion than a crane :
Therefore I beg I may return to England.

KING.

Sir Thomas, now I understand your mirth,
Which often plays with wisdom for its pastime,
And brings good counsel from the breast of
    laughter.
I hope you'll stay and see us fight this battle,
And reap rich harvest in the fields of Cressy ;
Then go to England, tell them how we fight,
And set all hearts on fire to be with us.
Philip is plumed, and thinks we flee from him,
Else he would never dare to attack us.   Now,
Now the quarry's set ! and death doth sport
In the bright sunshine of this fatal day.

DAGWORTH.

Now my heart dances, and I am as light
As the young bridegroom going to be married.
Now must I to my soldiers, get them ready,
Furbish our armours bright, new-plume our helms ;
And we will sing like the young housewives busied
In the dairy.   My feet are wing'd, but not
For flight, an please your grace.

KING.

If all my soldiers are as pleased as you,
'Twill be a gallant thing to fight or die ;
Then I can never be afraid of Philip.

DAGWORTH.

A raw-boned fellow t'other day passed by me ;
I told him to put off his hungry looks—
He answered me, " I hunger for another battle."
I saw a little Welshman with a fiery face ;
I told him he looked like a candle half
Burned out ; he answered, he was "*pig* enough
To light another *pattle*."   Last night, beneath
The moon I walked abroad, when all had pitched
Their tents, and all were still ;
I heard a blooming youth singing a song
He had composed, and at each pause he wiped
His dropping eyes.   The ditty was, " If he
Returned victorious, he should wed a maiden
Fairer than snow, and rich as midsummer."
Another wept, and wished health to his father.
I chid them both, but gave them noble hopes.

These are the minds that glory in the battle,
And leap and dance to hear the trumpet sound.

KING.

Sir Thomas Dagworth, be thou near our person ;
Thy heart is richer than the vales of France :
I will not part with such a man as thee.
If Philip came armed in the ribs of death,
And shook his mortal dart against my head,
Thou'dst laugh his fury into nerveless shame !
Go now, for thou art suited to the work
Throughout the camp : inflame the timorous,
Blow up the sluggish into ardour, and
Confirm the strong with strength, the weak inspire,
And wing their brows with hope and expectation :
Then to our tent return, and meet to council.

[*Exit* DAGWORTH.

CHANDOS.

That man's a hero in his closet, and more
A hero to the servants of his house
Than to the gaping world ; he carries windows
In that enlargèd breast of his, that all
May see what's done within.

PRINCE.

He is a genuine Englishman, my Chandos,
And hath the spirit of Liberty within him.
Forgive my prejudice, Sir John ; I think
My Englishmen the bravest people on
The face of the earth.

CHANDOS.

Courage, my Lord, proceeds from self-dependence.
Teach man to think he's a free agent,
Give but a slave his liberty, he'll shake
Off sloth, and build himself a hut, and hedge
A spot of ground ; this he'll defend ; 'tis his
By right of Nature.   Thus set in action,
He will still move onward to plan conveniences,
Till glory fires his breast to enlarge his castle ;
While the poor slave drudges all day, in hope
To rest at night.

KING.

O Liberty, how glorious art thou !
I see thee hovering o'er my army, with

Thy wide-stretched plumes ; I see thee
Lead them on to battle ;
I see thee blow thy golden trumpet while
Thy sons shout the strong shout of victory !
O noble Chandos, think thyself a gardener,
My son a vine, which I commit unto
Thy care.   Prune all extravagant shoots, and guide
The ambitious tendrils in the path of wisdom ;
Water him with thy advice, and heaven
Rain freshening dew upon his branches !   And,
O Edward, my dear son ! learn to think lowly of
Thyself, as we may all each prefer other—
'Tis the best policy, and 'tis our duty.

                              [*Exit* KING EDWARD.

PRINCE.

And may our duty, Chandos, be our pleasure.—
Now we are alone, Sir John, I will unburden
And breathe my hopes into the burning air,
Where thousand Deaths are posting up and down,
Commissioned to this fatal field of Cressy.
Methinks I see them arm my gallant soldiers,
And gird the sword upon each thigh, and fit

Each shining helm, and string each stubborn bow,
And dance to the neighing of our steeds.
Methinks the shout begins, the battle burns ;
Methinks I see them perch on English crests,
And roar the wild flame of fierce war upon
The throngèd enemy !   In truth, I am too full ;
It is my sin to love the noise of war.
Chandos, thou seest my weakness ; strong Nature
Will bend or break us : my blood, like a springtide,
Does rise so high to overflow all bounds
Of moderation ; while Reason, in her frail bark,
Can see no shore or bound for vast ambition.
Come, take the helm, my Chandos,
That my full-blown sails overset me not
In the wild tempest. Condemn my venturous youth,
That plays with danger, as the innocent child,
Unthinking, plays upon the viper's den :
I am a coward in my reason, Chandos.

CHANDOS.

You are a man, my prince, and a brave man,
If I can judge of actions ; but your heat
Is the effect of youth, and want of use :

Use makes the armèd field and noisy war
Pass over as a summer cloud, unregarded,
Or but expected as a thing of course.
Age is contemplative ; each rolling year
Brings forth fruit to the mind's treasure-house :
While vacant youth doth crave and seek about
Within itself, and findeth discontent,
Then, tired of thought, impatient takes the wing,
Seizes the fruits of time, attacks experience,
Roams round vast Nature's forest, where no bounds
Are set, the swiftest may have room, the strongest
Find prey ; till, tired at length, sated and tired
With the changing sameness, old variety,
We sit us down, and view our former joys
With distaste and dislike.

PRINCE.

Then, if we must tug for experience,
Let us not fear to beat round Nature's wilds,
And rouse the strongest prey : then, if we fall,
We fall with glory.   I know the wolf
Is dangerous to fight, not good for food,
Nor is the hide a comely vestment ; so

We have our battle for our pains.   I know
That youth has need of age to point fit prey,
And oft the stander-by shall steal the fruit
Of the other's labour.   This is philosophy ;
These are the tricks of the world ; but the pure
    soul
Shall mount on native wings, disdaining little sport,
And cut a path into the heaven of glory,
Leaving a track of light for men to wonder at.
I'm glad my father does not hear me talk ;
You can find friendly excuses for me, Chandos.
But do you not think, Sir John, that, if it please
The Almighty to stretch out my span of life,
I shall with pleasure view a glorious action
Which my youth mastered ?

CHANDOS.

Considerate age, my Lord, views motives,
And not acts ; when neither warbling voice
Nor trilling pipe is heard, nor pleasure sits
With trembling age, the voice of Conscience then,
Sweeter than music in a summer's eve,
Shall warble round the snowy head, and keep,

Sweet symphony to feathered angels, sitting
As guardians round your chair ; then shall the
    pulse
Beat slow, and taste and touch and sight and sound
    and smell,
That sing and dance round Reason's fine-wrought
    throne,
Shall flee away, and leave him all forlorn ;
Yet not forlorn if Conscience is his friend.

                                          [*Exeunt.*

SCENE.--*In* SIR THOMAS DAGWORTH'S *Tent.*

DAGWORTH *and* WILLIAM, *his man.*

DAGWORTH.

Bring hither my armour, William.
Ambition is the growth of every clime.

WILLIAM.

Does it grow in England, sir ?

DAGWORTH.

Ay, it grows most in lands most cultivated.

WILLIAM.

Then it grows most in France ; the vines here
Are finer than any we have in England.

DAGWORTH.

Ay, but the oaks are not.

WILLIAM.

What is the tree you mentioned ?   I don't think
I ever saw it.

DAGWORTH.

Ambition.

WILLIAM.

Is it a little creeping root that grows in ditches ?

DAGWORTH.

Thou dost not understand me, William.

H

It is a root that grows in every breast ;
Ambition is the desire or passion that one man
Has to get before another, in any pursuit after
    glory ;
But I don't think you have any of it.

WILLIAM.

Yes, I have ; I have a great ambition to know
everything, sir.

DAGWORTH.

But, when our first ideas are wrong, what follows
must all be wrong, of course ; 'tis best to know a
little, and to know that little aright.

WILLIAM.

Then, sir, I should be glad to know if it was not
ambition that brought over our king to France to
fight for his right.

DAGWORTH.

Though the knowledge of that will not profit thee
much, yet I will tell you that it *was* ambition.

WILLIAM.

Then, if ambition is a sin, we are all guilty in coming with him, and in fighting for him.

DAGWORTH.

Now, William, thou dost thrust the question home : but I must tell you that, guilt being an act of the mind, none are guilty but those whose minds are prompted by that same ambition.

WILLIAM.

Now, I always thought that a man might be guilty of doing wrong without knowing it was wrong.

DAGWORTH.

Thou art a natural philosopher, and knowst truth by instinct ; while reason runs aground, as we have run our argument. Only remember, William, all have it in their power to know the motives of their own actions, and 'tis a sin to act without some reason.

WILLIAM.

And whoever acts without reason may do a great deal of harm without knowing it.

DAGWORTH.

Thou art an endless moralist.

WILLIAM.

Now there's a story come into my head, that I will tell your honour, if you'll give me leave.

DAGWORTH.

No, William, save it till another time ; this is no time for story-telling.   But here comes one who is as entertaining as a good story.

Enter PETER BLUNT.

PETER.

Yonder's a musician going to play before the King; it's a new song about the French and English.   And the Prince has made the minstrel a squire, and given him I don't know what, and I can't tell whether he don't mention us all one by one ; and he is to write another about all us that are to die, that we may be remembered in Old England, for all our blood and bones are in France ; and a great deal more that we shall all hear by-and-by. And I came to tell your honour, because you love to hear war-songs.

DAGWORTH.

And who is this minstrel, Peter, dost know ?

PETER.

Oh, ay, I forgot to tell that ; he has got the same name as Sir John Chandos that the Prince is always with—the wise man that knows us all as well as your honour, only ain't so good-natured.

DAGWORTH.

I thank you, Peter, for your information, but not for your compliment, which is not true. There's as much difference between him and me as between glittering sand and fruitful mould; or shining glass and a wrought diamond, set in rich gold, and fitted to the finger of an Emperor; such is that worthy Chandos.

PETER.

I know your honour does not think anything of yourself, but everybody else does.

DAGWORTH.

Go, Peter, get you gone; flattery is delicious, even from the lips of a babbler.

[*Exit* PETER.

WILLIAM.

I never flatter your honour.

DAGWORTH.

I don't know that.

WILLIAM.

Why, you know, sir, when we were in England, at the tournament at Windsor, and the Earl of

Warwick was tumbled over, you asked me if he did not look well when he fell ; and I said no, he looked very foolish ; and you were very angry with me for not flattering you.

DAGWORTH.

You mean that I was angry with you for not flattering the Earl of Warwick.

[*Exeunt.*

SCENE.—*Sir Thomas Dagworth's Tent.*

Sir Thomas Dagworth. *To him enters* Sir Walter Manny.

SIR WALTER.

Sir Thomas Dagworth, I have been weeping
Over the men that are to die to-day.

DAGWORTH.

Why, brave Sir Walter, you or I may fall.

SIR WALTER.

I know this breathing flesh must lie and rot,
Covered with silence and forgetfulness.
Death roams in cities' smoke, and in still night,
When men sleep in their beds, walketh about.
How many in walled cities lie and groan,
Turning themselves upon their beds,
Talking with Death, answering his hard demands !
How many walk in darkness, terrors are round
The curtains of their beds, destruction is
Ready at the door !   How many sleep
In earth, covered with stones and deathy dust,
Resting in quietness, whose spirits walk
Upon the clouds of heaven, to die no more !
Yet death is terrible, though borne on angels'
       wings.
How terrible then is the field of death.
Where he doth rend the vault of heaven,
And shake the gates of hell !
O Dagworth, France is sick ! the very sky,
Though sunshine light it, seems to me as pale
As the pale fainting man on his death-bed,
Whose face is shown by light of sickly taper.

It makes me sad and sick at very heart ;
Thousands must fall to-day.

DAGWORTH.

Thousands of souls must leave this prison-house,
To be exalted to those heavenly fields
Where songs of triumph, palms of victory,
Where peace and joy and love and calm content,
Sit singing in the azure clouds, and strew
Flowers of heaven's growth over the banquet-table.
Bind ardent hope upon your feet like shoes,
Put on the robe of preparation !
The table is prepared in shining heaven,
The flowers of immortality are blown ;
Let those that fight fight in good steadfastness,
And those that fall shall rise in victory.

SIR WALTER.

I've often seen the burning field of war,
And often heard the dismal clang of arms ;
But never, till this fatal day of Cressy,
Has my soul fainted with these views of death.
I seem to be in one great charnel-house,

And seem to scent the rotten carcases ;
I seem to hear the dismal yells of Death,
While the black gore drops from his horrid jaws :
Yet I fear not the monster in his pride—
But oh ! the souls that are to die to-day !

DAGWORTH.

Stop, brave Sir Walter ; let me drop a tear,
Then let the clarion of war begin ;
I'll fight and weep, 'tis in my country's cause ;
I'll weep and shout for glorious liberty.
Grim War shall laugh and shout, decked in tears,
And blood shall flow like streams across the
      meadows,
That murmur down their pebbly channels, and
Spend their sweet lives to do their country service :
Then shall England's verdure shoot, her fields shall
      smile,
Her ships shall sing across the foaming sea,
Her mariners shall use the flute and viol,
And rattling guns, and black and dreary war,
Shall be no more.

SIR WALTER.

Well, let the trumpet sound, and the drum beat ;
Let war stain the blue heavens with bloody
    banners ;
I'll draw my sword, nor ever sheathe it up
Till England blow the trump of victory,
Or I lie stretched upon the field of death.

                        [Exeunt.

SCENE.—*In the Camp.*

*Several of the Warriors meet at the King's Tent
  with a Minstrel, who sings the following Song :*

O sons of Trojan Brutus, clothed in war,
Whose voices are the thunder of the field,
Rolling dark clouds o'er France, muffling the sun
In sickly darkness like a dim eclipse,
Threatening as the red brow of storms, as fire
Burning up nations in your wrath and fury !

Your ancestors came from the fires of Troy
(Like lions roused by lightning from their dens,
Whose eyes do glare against the stormy fires),

Heated with war, filled with the blood of Greeks,
With helmets hewn, and shields covered with gore,
In navies black, broken with wind and tide :

They landed in firm array upon the rocks
Of Albion ; they kissed the rocky shore ;
" Be thon our mother and our nurse," they said :
" Our children's mother, and thou shalt be our
    grave,
The sepulchre of Ancient Troy, from whence
Shall rise cities, and thrones, and arms, and awful
    powers."

Our fathers swarm from the ships.   Giant voices
Are heard from the hills, the enormous sons
Of Ocean run from rocks and caves ; wild men,
Naked and roaring like lions, hurling rocks,
And wielding knotty clubs, like oaks entangled
Thick as a forest, ready for the axe.

Our fathers move in firm array to battle ;
The savage monsters rush like roaring fire ;
Like as a forest roars with crackling flames,

When the red lightning, borne by furious storms,
Lights on some woody shore ; the parched heavens
Rain fire into the molten raging sea.

The smoking trees are strewn upon the shore,
Spoiled of their verdure.   Oh how oft have they
Defied the storm that howled o'er their heads !
Our fathers, sweating, lean on their spears, and view
The mighty dead : giant bodies streaming blood,
Dread visages frowning in silent death.

Then Brutus spoke, inspired ; our fathers sit
Attentive on the melancholy shore :
Hear ye the voice of Brutus—" The flowing waves
Of time come rolling o'er my breast," he said ;
" And my heart labours with futurity.
Our sons shall rule the empire of the sea.

" Their mighty wings shall stretch from east to west,
Their nest is in the sea, but they shall roam
Like eagles for the prey ; nor shall the young
Crave or be heard ; for plenty shall bring forth,

Cities shall sing, and vales in rich array
Shall laugh, whose fruitful laps bend down with
    fulness.

"Our sons shall rise from thrones in joy,
Each one buckling on his armour ; Morning
Shall be prevented by their swords gleaming,
And Evening hear their song of victory :
Their towers shall be built upon the rocks,
Their daughters shall sing, surrounded with shining
    spears.

"Liberty shall stand upon the cliffs of Albion,
Casting her blue eyes over the green ocean ;
Or towering stand upon the roaring waves,
Stretching her mighty spear o'er distant lands ;
While with her eagle wings she covereth
Fair Albion's shore, and all her families."

PROLOGUE.

INTENDED FOR A DRAMATIC PIECE OF KING
EDWARD THE FOURTH.

OH for a voice like thunder, and a tongue
    To drown the throat of war! When the
    senses
Are shaken, and the soul is driven to madness,
Who can stand? When the souls of the oppressed
Fight in the troubled air that rages, who can stand?
When the whirlwind of fury comes from the throne
Of God, when the frowns of His countenance
Drive the nations together, who can stand?
When Sin claps his broad wings over the battle,
And sails rejoicing in the flood of death ;
When souls are torn to everlasting fire,
And fiends of hell rejoice upon the slain,
Oh who can stand? Oh who hath caused this?
Oh who can answer at the throne of God?
The Kings and Nobles of the land have done it !
Hear it not, Heaven, thy ministers have done it !

PROLOGUE TO KING JOHN.

JUSTICE hath heaved a sword to plunge in
    Albion's breast ;
For Albion's sins are crimson-dyed,
And the red scourge follows her desolate sons.
Then Patriot rose ; full oft did Patriot rise,
When Tyranny hath stained fair Albion's breast
With her own children's gore.
Round his majestic feet deep thunders roll ;
Each heart does tremble, and each knee grows
    slack.   [war,
The stars of heaven tremble ; the roaring voice of
The trumpet, calls to battle. Brother in brother's
    blood
Must bathe, rivers of death.   O land most hapless !
O beauteous island, how forsaken !
Weep from thy silver fountains, weep from thy
    gentle rivers !
The angel of the island weeps ;
The widowed virgins weep beneath thy shades.
Thy aged fathers gird themselves for war ;

The sucking infant lives, to die in battle ;
The weeping mother feeds him for the slaughter.
The husbandman doth leave his bending harvest.
Blood cries afar !   The land doth sow itself !
The glittering youth of courts must gleam in arms ;
The aged senators their ancient swords assume ;
The trembling sinews of old age must work
The work of death against their progeny.
For Tyranny hath stretched his purple arm,
And " Blood ! " he cries : " The chariots and the
    horses,
The noise of shout, and dreadful thunder of the
    battle heard afar ! "
Beware, O proud ! thou shalt be humbled ;
Thy cruel brow, thine iron heart is smitten,
Though lingering Fate is slow.   O yet may Albion
Smile again, and stretch her peaceful arms,
And raise her golden head exultingly !
Her citizens shall throng about her gates,
Her mariners shall sing upon the sea,
And myriads shall to her temples crowd !
Her sons shall joy as in the morning—
Her daughters sing as to the rising year !

I

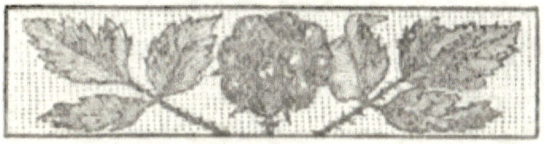

SONGS OF INNOCENCE.

(ENGRAVED 1789.)

INTRODUCTION.

PIPING down the valleys wild,
　　Piping songs of pleasant glee,
On a cloud I saw a child,
　　And he laughing said to me :

"Pipe a song about a Lamb ! "
　　So I piped with merry cheer.
" Piper, pipe that song again ; "
　　So I piped : he wept to hear.

" Drop thy pipe, thy happy pipe ;
　　Sing thy songs of happy cheer ! "

So I sang the same again,
    While he wept with joy to hear.

" Piper, sit thee down and write
    In a book that all may read."
So he vanished from my sight ;
    And I plucked a hollow reed,

And I made a rural pen,
    And I stained the water clear,
And I wrote my happy songs
    Every child my joy to hear.

THE SHEPHERD.

HOW sweet is the shepherd's sweet lot !
    From the morn to the evening he strays ;
He shall follow his sheep all the day,
And his tongue shall be filled with praise.

For he hears the lambs' innocent call,
And he hears the ewes' tender reply ;
He is watchful while they are in peace,
For they know when their shepherd is nigh.

THE ECHOING GREEN.

THE sun does arise,
    And make happy the skies ;
The merry bells ring,
To welcome the Spring ;
The skylark and thrush,
The birds of the bush,
Sing louder around
To the bells' cheerful sound ;

While our sports shall be seen
On the echoing green.

Old John, with white hair,
Does laugh away care,
Sitting under the oak,
Among the old folk.
They laugh at our play,
And soon they all say,
" Such, such were the joys
When we all—girls and boys—
In our youth-time were seen
On the echoing green."

Till the little ones, weary,
No more can be merry :
The sun does descend,
And our sports have an end.
Round the laps of their mothers
Many sisters and brothers,
Like birds in their nest,
Are ready for rest,
And sport no more seen
On the darkening green.

THE LAMB.

LITTLE lamb, who made thee?
    Dost thou know who made thee,
Gave thee life, and bade thee feed
By the stream and o'er the mead;
Gave thee clothing of delight,
Softest clothing, woolly, bright;
Gave thee such a tender voice,
Making all the vales rejoice?
    Little lamb, who made thee?
    Dost thou know who made thee?

    Little lamb, I'll tell thee;
    Little lamb, I'll tell thee:
He is callèd by thy name,
For He calls himself a lamb.
He is meek, and He is mild,
He became a little child.
I a child, and thou a lamb,
We are callèd by His name.
    Little lamb, God bless thee!
    Little lamb, God bless thee!

THE LITTLE BLACK BOY.

MY mother bore me in the southern wild,
 And I am black, but oh my soul is white,
White as an angel is the English child,
 But I am black, as if bereaved of light.

My mother taught me underneath a tree,
 And, sitting down before the heat of day,
She took me on her lap and kissèd me,
 And, pointing to the East, began to say:

" Look on the rising sun : there God does live,
 And gives his light, and gives his heat away,
And flowers and trees and beasts and men receive
 Comfort in morning, joy in the noonday.

" And we are put on earth a little space,
 That we may learn to bear the beams of love ;
And these black bodies and this sunburnt face
 Are but a cloud, and like a shady grove.

" For, when our souls have learned the heat to
　　bear,
　The cloud will vanish, we shall hear his voice,
Saying, ' Come out from the grove, my love and
　　care,
　And round my golden tent like lambs rejoice.' "

Thus did my mother say, and kissèd me,
　And thus I say to little English boy.
When I from black, and he from white cloud free,
　And round the tent of God like lambs we joy,

I'll shade him from the heat till he can bear
　To lean in joy upon our Father's knee ;
And then I'll stand and stroke his silver hair,
　And be like him, and he will then love me.

THE BLOSSOM.

MERRY, merry sparrow !
　　Under leaves so green
A happy blossom
Sees you, swift as arrow,
Seek your cradle narrow,
Near my bosom.

Pretty, pretty robin !
Under leaves so green
A happy blossom
Hears you sobbing, sobbing,
Pretty, pretty robin,
Near my bosom.

———

THE CHIMNEY-SWEEPER.

WHEN my mother died I was very young,
　　And my father sold me while yet my tongue
Could scarcely cry, " Weep ! weep ! weep ! weep !"
So your chimneys I sweep, and in soot I sleep.

There's little Tom Dacre, who cried when his
    head,
That curled like a lamb's back, was shaved ; so I
    said,
" Hush, Tom ! never mind it, for, when your head's
    bare,
You know that the soot cannot spoil your white
    hair."

And so he was quiet, and that very night,
As Tom was a-sleeping, he had such a sight !—
That thousands of sweepers, Dick, Joe, Ned, and
    Jack,
Were all of them locked up in coffins of black.

And by came an angel, who had a bright key,
And he opened the coffins and set them all free ;
Then down a green plain, leaping, laughing, they
    run,
And wash in a river, and shine in the sun.

Then naked and white, all their bags left behind,
They rise upon clouds, and sport in the wind ;

And the angel told Tom, if he'd be a good boy,
He'd have God for his father, and never want joy.

And so Tom awoke, and we rose in the dark,
And got with our bags and our brushes to work.
Though the morning was cold, Tom was happy
and warm :
So if all do their duty, they need not fear harm.

THE LITTLE BOY LOST.

" FATHER, father, where are you going ?
Oh do not walk so fast !
Speak, father, speak to your little boy,
Or else I shall be lost."

The night was dark, no father was there,
The child was wet with dew ;
The mire was deep, and the child did weep,
And away the vapour flew.

THE LITTLE BOY FOUND.

THE little boy lost in the lonely fen,
    Led by the wandering light,
Began to cry, but God, ever nigh,
    Appeared like his father, in white.

He kissed the child, and by the hand led,
    And to his mother brought,
Who in sorrow pale, through the lonely dale,
    The little boy weeping sought.

LAUGHING SONG.

WHEN the green woods laugh with the voice
      of joy,
And the dimpling stream runs laughing by;
When the air does laugh with our merry wit,
And the green hill laughs with the noise of it;

When the meadows laugh with lively green,
And the grasshopper laughs in the merry scene ;
When Mary, and Susan, and Emily
With their sweet round mouths sing, " Ha, ha, he ! "

When the painted birds laugh in the shade,
Where our table with cherries and nuts is spread :
Come live, and be merry, and join with me,
To sing the sweet chorus of " Ha, ha, he ! "

A CRADLE SONG.

SWEET dreams, form a shade
   O'er my lovely infant's head !
Sweet dreams of pleasant streams
By happy, silent, moony beams !

Sweet sleep, with soft down
Weave thy brows an infant crown !
Sweet sleep, angel mild,
Hover o'er my happy child !

Sweet smiles, in the night
Hover over my delight !
Sweet smiles, mother's smile,
All the livelong night beguile.

Sweet moans, dovelike sighs,
Chase not slumber from thine eyes !
Sweet moan, sweeter smile,
All the dovelike moans beguile

Sleep, sleep, happy child !
All creation slept and smiled.
Sleep, sleep, happy sleep,
While o'er thee doth mother weep.

Sweet babe, in thy face
Holy image I can trace ;
Sweet babe, once like thee
Thy Maker lay, and wept for me :

Wept for me, for thee, for all,
When He was an infant small.
Thou His image ever see,
Heavenly face that smiles on thee !

Smiles on thee, on me, on all,
Who became an infant small ;
Infant smiles are His own smiles :
Heaven and earth to peace beguiles.

THE DIVINE IMAGE.

TO Mercy, Pity, Peace, and Love,
  All pray in their distress,
And to these virtues of delight
  Return their thankfulness.

For Mercy, Pity, Peace, and Love,
  Is God our Father dear ;
And Mercy, Pity, Peace, and Love,
  Is man, his child and care.

For Mercy has a human heart ;
  Pity, a human face ;
And Love, the human form divine ;
  And Peace, the human dress.

Then every man, of every clime,
  That prays in his distress,
Prays to the human form divine :
  Love, Mercy, Pity, Peace.

And all must love the human form,
  In heathen, Turk, or Jew.
Where Mercy, Love, and Pity dwell,
  There God is dwelling too.

HOLY THURSDAY.

'TWAS on a Holy Thursday, their innocent
    faces clean,
Came children walking two and two, in red, and
  blue, and green :
Grey-headed beadles walked before, with wands as
  white as snow,
Till into the high dome of Paul's they like Thames
  waters flow.

Oh what a multitude they seemed, these flowers of
  London town !
Seated in companies they sit, with radiance all
  their own.
The hum of multitudes was there, but multitudes of
  lambs,
Thousands of little boys and girls raising their
  innocent hands.

Now like a mighty wind they raise to heaven the
  voice of song,
Or like harmonious thunderings the seats of heaven
  among :
Beneath them sit the aged men, wise guardians of
  the poor.
Then cherish pity, lest you drive an angel from
  your door.

NIGHT.

THE sun descending in the west,
 The evening star does shine .
The birds are silent in their nest,
And I must seek for mine.
 The moon like a flower
 In heaven's high bower,
 With silent delight,
 Sits and smiles on the night.

Farewell, green fields and happy grove,
Where flocks have ta'en delight.
Where lambs have nibbled, silent move
The feet of angels bright ;
 Unseen, they pour blessing,
 And joy without ceasing,
 On each bud and blossom,
 And each sleeping bosom.

They look in every thoughtless nest
Where birds are covered warm ;

They visit caves of every beast,
To keep them all from harm :
  If they see any weeping
  That should have been sleeping,
  They pour sleep on their head,
  And sit down by their bed.

When wolves and tigers howl for prey,
They pitying stand and weep,
Seeking to drive their thirst away,
And keep them from the sheep.
  But, if they rush dreadful,
  The angels, most heedful,
  Receive each mild spirit,
  New worlds to inherit.

And there the lion's ruddy eyes
Shall flow with tears of gold :
And pitying the tender cries,
And walking round the fold :
  Saying : " Wrath by His meekness,
  And, by His health, sickness,

Are driven away
From our immortal day.

"And now beside thee, bleating lamb,
I can lie down and sleep,
Or think on Him who bore thy name,
Graze after thee, and weep.
    For, washed in life's river,
    My bright mane for ever
    Shall shine like the gold,
    As I guard o'er the fold."

SPRING.

SOUND the flute !
        Now 'tis mute ;
Birds delight,
Day and night,
Nightingale,
In the dale,
Lark in sky—
Merrily,
Merrily, merrily to welcome in the year.

Little boy,
Full of joy ;
Little girl,
Sweet and small,
Cock does crow,
So do you ;
Merry voice,
Infant noise ;
Merrily, merrily to welcome in the year.

Little lamb,
Here I am ;
Come and lick
My white neck ;
Let me pull
Your soft wool ;
Let me kiss
Your soft face ;
Merrily, merrily we welcome in the year.

NURSE'S SONG.

WHEN the voices of children are heard on the
    green,
  And laughing is heard on the hill,
My heart is at rest within my breast,
  And everything else is still.
"Then come home, my children, the sun is gone
    down,
  And the dews of night arise ;
Come, come, leave off play, and let us away,
  Till the morning appears in the skies."

"No, no, let us play, for it is yet day,
  And we cannot go to sleep ;
Besides, in the sky the little birds fly,
  And the hills are all covered with sheep."
"Well, well, go and play till the light fades away,
  And then go home to bed."
The little ones leaped, and shouted, and laughed,
  And all the hills echoèd.

INFANT JOY.

" I HAVE no name ;
    I am but two days old."
What shall I call thee?
" I happy am,
Joy is my name,"
Sweet joy befall thee !

Pretty joy !
Sweet joy, but two days old.
Sweet joy I call thee ;
Thou dost smile,
I sing the while ;
Sweet joy befall thee !

A DREAM.

ONCE a dream did weave a shade
    O'er my angel-guarded bed,
That an emmet lost its way
Where on grass methought I lay.

Troubled, wildered, and forlorn,
Dark, benighted, travel-worn,
Over many a tangled spray,
All heart-broke, I heard her say :

"Oh, my children ! do they cry,
Do they hear their father sigh ?
Now they look abroad to see,
Now return and weep for me."

Pitying, I dropped a tear :
But I saw a glow-worm near,
Who replied, " What wailing wight
Calls the watchman of the night ?

" I am set to light the ground,
While the beetle goes his round :
Follow now the beetle's hum ;
Little wanderer, hie thee home ! "

ON ANOTHER'S SORROW.

CAN I see another's woe,
    nd not be in sorrow too?
Can I see another's grief,
And not seek for kind relief?

Can I see a falling tear,
And not feel my sorrow's share?
Can a father see his child
Weep, nor be with sorrow filled?

Can a mother sit and hear
An infant groan, an infant fear?
No, no! never can it be!
Never, never can it be!

And can He who smiles on all
Hear the wren with sorrows small,
Hear the small bird's grief and care
Hear the woes that infants bear—

And not sit beside the nest,
Pouring pity in their breast,

And not sit the cradle near,
Weeping tear on infant's tear?

And not sit both night and day,
Wiping all our tears away?
Oh no! never can it be!
Never, never can it be!

He doth give His joy to all:
He becomes an Infant small,
He becomes a Man of Woe,
He doth feel the sorrow too.

Think not thou canst sigh a sigh,
And thy Maker is not by:
Think not thou canst weep a tear,
And thy Maker is not near.

Oh, He gives to us His joy,
That our grief He may destroy:
Till our grief is fled and gone
He doth sit by us and moan.

THE VOICE OF THE ANCIENT BARD.

YOUTH of delight ! come hither
    And see the opening morn,
Image of Truth new-born.
Doubt is fled, and clouds of reason,
Dark disputes and artful teazing.
Folly is an endless maze ;
Tangled roots perplex her ways ;
How many have fallen there !
They stumble all night over bones of the dead ;
And feel—they know not what, but care ;
And wish to lead others, when they should be led.

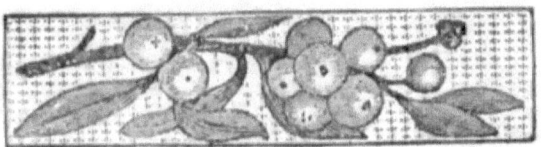

SONGS OF EXPERIENCE.

(ENGRAVED 1794.)

INTRODUCTION.

HEAR the voice of the Bard,
    Who present, past, and future sees ;
Whose ears have heard
The Holy Word
That walked among the ancient trees ;

Calling the lapsèd soul,
And weeping in the evening dew ;
That might control
The starry pole,
And fallen, fallen light renew !

"O Earth, O Earth, return !
Arise from out the dewy grass !
Night is worn,
And the morn
Rises from the slumb'rous mass.

"Turn away no more ;
Why wilt thou turn away ?
The starry floor,
The watery shore,
Are given thee till the break of day."

EARTH'S ANSWER.

EARTH raised up her head
From the darkness dread and drear,
Her light fled,
Stony, dread,
And her locks covered with grey despair.

"Prisoned on watery shore,
Starry jealousy does keep my den
Cold and hoar :
Weeping o'er,
I hear the father of the ancient men,

"Selfish father of men !
Cruel, jealous, selfish fear !
Can delight,
Chained in night,
The virgins of youth and morning bear ?

"Does spring hide its joy,
When buds and blossoms grow ?
Does the sower
Sow by night,
Or the ploughman in darkness plough ?

"Break this heavy chain,
That does freeze my bones around !
Selfish, vain,
Eternal bane,
That free love with bondage bound."

THE CLOD AND THE PEBBLE.

" L OVE seeketh not itself to please,
    Nor for itself hath any care,
But for another gives its ease,
    And builds a heaven in hell's despair."

So sang a little clod of clay,
    Trodden with the cattle's feet.
But a pebble of the brook
    Warbled out these metres meet :

" Love seeketh only *Self* to please,
    To bind another to its delight,
Joys in another's loss of ease,
    And builds a hell in heaven's despite."

HOLY THURSDAY. ✓

IS this a holy thing to see
　　In a rich and fruitful land—
Babes reduced to misery,
　　Fed with cold and usurous hand?

Is that trembling cry a song?
　　Can it be a song of joy?
And so many children poor?
　　It is a land of poverty!

And their sun does never shine, ✓
　　And their fields are bleak and bare,
And their ways are filled with thorns:
　　It is eternal winter there.

For where'er the sun does shine,
　　And where'er the rain does fall,
Babes should never hunger there,
　　Nor poverty the mind appal.

THE LITTLE GIRL LOST.

I N futurity
    I prophetic see
That the earth from sleep
(Grave the sentence deep)

Shall arise and seek
For her Maker meek ;
And the desert wild
Become a garden mild.

In the southern clime,
Where the Summer's prime
Never fades away,
Lovely Lyca lay.

Seven summers old
Lovely Lyca told.
She had wandered long,
Hearing wild birds' song.

L

"Sweet sleep, come to me
Underneath this tree ;
Do father, mother, weep?
Where can Lyca sleep?

" Lost in desert wild
Is your little child.
How can Lyca sleep
If her mother weep?

" If her heart does ache,
Then let Lyca wake ;
If my mother sleep,
Lyca shall not weep.

" Frowning, frowning night,
O'er this desert bright
Let thy moon arise,
While I close my eyes."

Sleeping Lyca lay
While the beasts of prey,
Come from caverns deep,
Viewed the maid asleep.

The kingly lion stood,
And the virgin viewed :
Then he gambolled round
O'er the hallowed ground.

Leopards, tigers play
Round her as she lay ;
While the lion old
Bowed his mane of gold,

And her breast did lick,
And upon her neck,
From his eyes of flame,
Ruby tears there came ;

While the lioness
Loosed her slender dress,
And naked they conveyed
To caves the sleeping maid.

THE LITTLE GIRL FOUND.

A LL the night in woe
    Lyca's parents go
Over valleys deep,
While the deserts weep.

Tired and woe-begone,
Hoarse with making moan,
Arm in arm, seven days
They traced the desert ways.

Seven nights they sleep
Among shadows deep,
And dream they see their child
Starved in desert wild.

Pale through pathless ways
The fancied image strays,
Famished, weeping, weak,
With hollow piteous shriek.

Rising from unrest,
The trembling woman pressed
With feet of weary woe ;
She could no further go.

In his arms he bore
Her, armed with sorrow sore ;
Till before their way
A crouching lion lay.

Turning back was vain :
Soon his heavy mane
Bore them to the ground.
Then he stalked around,

Smelling to his prey ;
But their fears allay
When he licks their hands,
And silent by them stands.

They look upon his eyes,
Filled with deep surprise ;
And wondering behold
A spirit armed in gold.

On his head a crown,
On his shoulders down
Flowed his golden hair.
Gone was all their care.

" Follow me," he said ;
" Weep not for the maid ;
In my palace deep
Lyca lies asleep."

Then they followèd
Where the vision led,
And saw their sleeping child
Among tigers wild.

To this day they dwell
In a lonely dell,
Nor fear the wolvish howl
Nor the lion's growl.

THE CHIMNEY SWEEPER.

A LITTLE black thing among the snow,
    Crying, " Weep ! weep ! " in notes of woe !
" Where are thy father and mother ?   Say ! "—
" They are both gone up to the church to pray.

" Because I was happy upon the heath,
And smiled among the winter's snow,
They clothed me in the clothes of death,
And taught me to sing the notes of woe.

" And because I am happy and dance and sing,
They think they have done me no injury,
And are gone to praise God and his priest and king,
Who make up a heaven of our misery."

THE SICK ROSE.

O ROSE, thou art sick !
    The invisible worm,
That flies in the night,
    In the howling storm,

Has found out thy bed
Of crimson joy,
And his dark secret love
Does thy life destroy.

NURSE'S SONG.

WHEN the voices of children are heard on the
        green,
  And whisperings are in the dale,
The days of my youth rise fresh in my mind,
  My face turns green and pale.

Then come home, my children, the sun is gone
        down,
  And the dews of night arise;
Your spring and your day are wasted in play,
  And your winter and night in disguise.

THE FLY.

L ITTLE Fly,
  Thy summer's play
My thoughtless hand
Has brushed away.

Am not I
A fly like thee?
Or art not thou
A man like me?

For I dance,
And drink, and sing,
Till some blind hand
Shall brush my wing.

If thought is life
And strength and breath,
And the want
Of thought is death ;

Then am I
A happy fly,
If I live,
Or if I die.

THE ANGEL.

I DREAMT a dream !   What can it mean ?
 And that I was a maiden Queen
Guarded by an Angel mild :
Witless woe was ne'er beguiled !

And I wept both night and day,
And he wiped my tears away ;
And I wept both day and night,
And hid from him my heart's delight.

So he took his wings, and fled ;
Then the morn blushed rosy red.
I dried my tears, and armed my fears
With ten thousand shields and spears.

Soon my Angel came again ;
I was armed, he came in vain ;
For the time of youth was fled,
And grey hairs were on my head.

THE TIGER.

TIGER, tiger, burning bright
   In the forests of the night,
What immortal hand or eye
Could frame thy fearful symmetry?

In what distant deeps or skies
Burnt the fire of thine eyes ?
On what wings dare he aspire ?
What the hand dare seize the fire ?

And what shoulder and what art
Could twist the sinews of thy heart ?
And, when thy heart began to beat,
What dread hand and what dread feet ?

What the hammer? what the chain?
In what furnace was thy brain?
What the anvil? what dread grasp
Dare its deadly terrors clasp?

When the stars threw down their spears,
And watered heaven with their tears,
Did He smile his work to see?
Did He who made the lamb make thee?

Tiger, tiger, burning bright
In the forests of the night,
What immortal hand or eye
Dare frame thy fearful symmetry?

MY PRETTY ROSE TREE.

A FLOWER was offered to me,
    Such a flower as May never bore;
But I said, " I've a pretty rose tree,"
    And I passed the sweet flower o'er.

Then I went to my pretty rose tree,
　To tend her by day and by night ;
But my rose turned away with jealousy,
　And her thorns were my only delight.

AH, SUNFLOWER.

AH, Sunflower, weary of time,
　Who countest the steps of the sun ;
Seeking after that sweet golden clime
　Where the traveller's journey is done ;

Where the Youth pined away with desire,
　And the pale virgin shrouded in snow,
Arise from their graves, and aspire
　Where my Sunflower wishes to go !

THE LILY.

THE modest Rose puts forth a thorn,
   The humble sheep a threat'ning horn ;
While the Lily white shall in love delight,
Nor a thorn nor a threat stain her beauty bright.

THE GARDEN OF LOVE.

I LAID me down upon a bank
   Where Love lay sleeping ;
I heard among the rushes dank
   Weeping, weeping.

Then I went to the heath and the wild,
   To the thistles and thorns of the waste ;
And they told me how they were beguiled,
   Driven out, and compelled to be chaste.

I went to the Garden of Love,
   And saw what I never had seen ;

A chapel was built in the midst,
  Where I used to play on the green.

And the gates of this chapel were shut,
  And " Thou shalt not " writ over the door ;
So I turned to the Garden of Love,
  That so many sweet flowers bore.

And I saw it was filled with graves,
  And tombstones where flowers should be ;
And priests in black gowns were walking their
    rounds,
And binding with briars my joys and desires.

THE LITTLE VAGABOND.

DEAR mother, dear mother, the Church is cold ;
  But the Alehouse is healthy, and pleasant,
    and warm.
Besides, I can tell where I am used well ;
The poor parsons with wind like a blown bladder
  swell.

But, if at the Church they would give us some ale,
And a pleasant fire our souls to regale,
We'd sing and we'd pray all the livelong day,
Nor ever once wish from the Church to stray.

Then the Parson might preach, and drink, and sing,
And we'd be as happy as birds in the spring ;
And modest Dame Lurch, who is always at church,
Would not have bandy children, nor fasting, nor birch.

And God, like a father, rejoicing to see
His children as pleasant and happy as he,
Would have no more quarrel with the Devil or the
        barrel,
But kiss him, and give him both drink and apparel.

LONDON.

I WANDER through each chartered street,
    Near where the chartered Thames does
  flow,
A mark in every face I meet—
    Marks of weakness, marks of woe.

In every cry of every man,
   In every infant's cry of fear,
In every voice, in every ban,
   The mind-forged manacles I hear:

How the chimney-sweeper's cry
   Every blackening church appals,
And the hapless soldier's sigh
   Runs in blood down palace-walls.

But most, through midnight streets I hear
   How the youthful harlot's curse
Blasts the new-born infant's tear,
   And blights with plagues the marriage-
      hearse.

———

THE HUMAN ABSTRACT.

PITY would be no more
   If we did not make somebody poor,
And Mercy no more could be
If all were as happy as we.

M

And mutual fear brings Peace,
Till the selfish loves increase ;
Then Cruelty knits a snare,
And spreads his baits with care.

He sits down with holy fears,
And waters the ground with tears ;
Then Humility takes its root
Underneath his foot.

Soon spreads the dismal shade
Of Mystery over his head,
And the caterpillar and fly
Feed on the Mystery.

And it bears the fruit of Deceit,
Ruddy and sweet to eat,
And the raven his nest has made
In its thickest shade.

The gods of the earth and sea
Sought through nature to find this tree,
But their search was all in vain :
There grows one in the human Brain.

INFANT SORROW.

MY mother groaned, my father wept :
    Into the dangerous world I leapt,
Helpless, naked, piping loud,
Like a fiend hid in a cloud.

Struggling in my father's hands
Striving against my swaddling-bands,
Bound and weary, I thought best
To sulk upon my mother's breast.

CHRISTIAN FORBEARANCE.

I WAS angry with my friend :
    I told my wrath, my wrath did end.
I was angry with my foe :
I told it not, my wrath did grow.

And I watered it in fears
Night and morning with my tears,

And I sunnèd it with smiles
And with soft deceitful wiles.

And it grew both day and night
Till it bore an apple bright,
And my foe beheld it shine,
And he knew that it was mine,—

And into my garden stole
When the night had veiled the pole ;
In the morning, glad, I see
My foe outstretched beneath the tree.

A LITTLE BOY LOST.

" NOUGHT loves another as itself,
        Nor venerates another so,
Nor is it possible to thought
    A greater than itself to know.

" And, father, how can I love you
    Or any of my brothers more ?

I love you like the little bird
   That picks up crumbs around the door."

The Priest sat by and heard the child ;
   In trembling zeal he seized his hair,
He led him by his little coat,
   And all admired the priestly care.

And standing on the altar high,
   " Lo, what a fiend is here !" said he ;
" One who sets reason up for judge
   Of our most holy mystery."

The weeping child could not be heard,
   The weeping parents wept in vain :
They stripped him to his little shirt,
   And bound him in an iron chain,

And burned him in a holy place
   Where many had been burned before ;
The weeping parents wept in vain.
   Are such things done on Albion's shore?

A LITTLE GIRL LOST.

CHILDREN of the future age,
    Reading this indignant page,
Know that in a former time
Love, sweet love, was thought a crime.

In the age of gold,
Free from winter's cold,
Youth and maiden bright,
To the holy light,
Naked in the sunny beams delight.

Once a youthful pair,
Filled with softest care,
Met in garden bright
Where the holy light
Had just removed the curtains of the night.

Then, in rising day,
On the grass they play ;
Parents were afar,
Strangers came not near,
And the maiden soon forgot her fear.

Tired with kisses sweet,
They agree to meet
When the silent sleep
Waves o'er heaven's deep,
And the weary tired wanderers weep.

To her father white
Came the maiden bright ;
But his loving look,
Like the holy book,
All her tender limbs with terror shook.

" Ona, pale and weak,
To thy father speak !
Oh, the trembling fear !
Oh, the dismal care
That shakes the blossoms of my hoary hair ! "

A DIVINE IMAGE.

CRUELTY has a human heart,
　　And Jealousy a human face ;
Terror the human form divine,
　　And Secrecy the human dress.

The human dress is forgèd iron,
　　The human form a fiery forge,
The human face a furnace sealed,
　　The human heart its hungry gorge.

THE SCHOOLBOY.

I LOVE to rise on a summer morn,
　　When birds are singing on every tree ;
The distant huntsman winds his horn,
　　And the skylark sings with me :
　　Oh what sweet company !

But to go to school in a summer morn—
  Oh, it drives all joy away !
Under a cruel eye outworn,
  The little ones spend the day
  In sighing and dismay.

Ah, then at times I drooping sit,
  And spend many an anxious hour ;
Nor in my book can I take delight,
  Nor sit in learning's bower,
  Worn through with the dreary shower.

How can the bird that is born for joy
  Sit in a cage and sing ?
How can a child, when fears annoy,
  But droop his tender wing,
  And forget his youthful spring ?

Ah, father and mother, if buds are nipped,
  And blossoms blown away ;
And if the tender plants are stripped
  Of their joy in the springing day,
  By sorrow and care's dismay—

How shall the summer arise in joy,
  Or the summer fruits appear?
Or how shall we gather what griefs destroy,
  Or bless the mellowing year,
  When the blasts of winter appear?

TO TIRZAH.

WHATE'ER is born of mortal birth
      Must be consumèd with the earth,
To rise from generation free :
Then what have I to do with thee?

The sexes sprang from shame and pride,
Blown in the morn, in evening died ;
But mercy changed death into sleep ;
The sexes rose to work and weep.

Thou, mother of my mortal part,
With cruelty didst mould my heart,
And with false self-deceiving tears
Didst bind my nostrils, eyes, and ears,

Didst close my tongue in senseless clay,
And me to mortal life betray.
The death of Jesus set me free:
Then what have I to do with thee?

THE BOOK OF THEL.

(ENGRAVED 1789.)

Does the Eagle know what is in the pit,
  Or wilt thou go ask the Mole?
Can wisdom be put in a silver rod,
  Or love in a golden bowl?

I.

THE Daughters of the Seraphim led round their
    sunny flocks—
All but the youngest : she in paleness sought the
    secret air,
To fade away like morning beauty from her mortal
    day.
Down by the river of Adona her soft voice is heard,
And thus her gentle lamentation falls like morning
    dew.

"O life of this our Spring! why fades the lotus of
  the water?
Why fade these children of the Spring, born but to
  smile and fall?
Ah! Thel is like a watery bow, and like a parting
  cloud,
Like a reflection in a glass, like shadows in the
  water,
Like dreams of infants, like a smile upon an
  infant's face,
Like the dove's voice, like transient day, like music
  in the air.
Ah! gentle may I lay me down, and gentle rest
  my head,
And gentle sleep the sleep of death, and gentle
  hear the voice
Of Him that walketh in the garden in the evening
  time!"

The Lily of the Valley, breathing in the humble
  grass,
Answered the lovely maid, and said: "I am a
  watery weed,

And I am very small, and love to dwell in lowly
    vales ;
So weak, the gilded butterfly scarce perches on my
    head.
Yet I am visited from heaven ; and He that smiles
    on all
Walks in the valley, and each morn over me
    spreads his hand,
Saying, 'Rejoice, thou humble grass, thou new-
    born lily-flower,
Thou gentle maid of silent valleys and of modest
    brooks ;
For thou shalt be clothed in light, and fed with
    morning manna,
Till summer's heat melts thee beside the fountains
    and the springs,
To flourish in eternal vales.' Then why should
    Thel complain ?
Why should the mistress of the vales of Har utter
    a sigh ? "

She ceased, and smiled in tears, then sat down in
    her silver shrine.

Thel answered : " O thou little virgin of the peaceful valley,
Giving to those that cannot crave, the voiceless,
  the o'ertired,
Thy breath doth nourish the innocent lamb ; he
  smells thy milky garments,
He crops thy flowers, while thou sittest smiling in
  his face,
Wiping his mild and meekin mouth from all con-
  tagious taints.
Thy wine doth purify the golden honey ; thy
  perfume,
Which thou dost scatter on every little blade of
  grass that springs,
Revives the milkèd cow, and tames the fire-
  breathing steed.
But Thel is like a faint cloud kindled at the rising
  sun :
I vanish from my pearly throne, and who shall find
  my place ?"

" Queen of the vales," the Lily answered, "ask the
  tender Cloud,

And it shall tell thee why it glitters in the morning
  sky,
And why it scatters its bright beauty through the
  humid air.
Descend, O little Cloud, and hover before the eyes
  of Thel."

The Cloud descended ; and the Lily bowed her
  modest head,
And went to mind her numerous charge among the
  verdant grass.

II.

" O little cloud," the virgin said, " I charge thee
  tell to me
Why thou complainest not, when in one hour thou
  fad'st away :
Then we shall seek thee, but not find.   Ah ! Thel
  is like to thee—
I pass away ; yet I complain, and no one hears my
  voice."

The Cloud then showed his golden head, and his
 bright form emerged,
Hovering and glittering on the air, before the face
 of Thel.

" O virgin, know'st thou not our steeds drink of the
 golden springs
Where Luvah doth renew his horses ! Look'st
 thou on my youth,
And fearest thou because I vanish and am seen no
 more ?
Nothing remains. O maid, I tell thee, when I
 pass away,
It is to tenfold life, to love, to peace, and raptures
 holy.
Unseen descending weigh my light wings upon
 balmy flowers,
And court the fair-eyed Dew to take me to her
 shining tent :
The weeping virgin trembling kneels before the
 risen sun,
Till we arise, linked in a golden band, and never
 part,

N

But walk united, bearing food to all our tender
 . flowers."

" Dost thou, O little Cloud?   I fear that I am not
    like thee ;
For I walk through the vales of Har, and smell the
    sweetest flowers,
But I feed not the little flowers : I hear the
    warbling birds,
But I feed not the warbling birds, they fly and
    seek their food.
But Thel delights in these no more ! because I
    fade away,
And all shall say, ' Without a use this shining
    woman lived,
Or did she only live to be at death the food of
    worms ? ' "

The Cloud reclined upon his airy throne, and
    answered thus :

" Then if thou art the food of worms, O virgin of
    the skies,

How great thy use, how great thy blessing ! Every
    thing that lives
Lives not alone nor for itself. Fear not, and I
    will call
The weak Worm from its lowly bed, and thou shalt
    hear its voice.
Come forth, Worm of the silent valley, to thy
    pensive queen."

The helpless Worm arose, and sat upon the Lily's
    leaf,
And the bright Cloud sailed on to find his partner
    in the vale.

III.

Then Thel, astonished, viewed the Worm upon its
    dewy bed.

" Art thou a worm, image of weakness? art thou
    but a worm ?
I see thee, like an infant, wrapped in the Lily's leaf.
Ah ! weep not, little voice ; thou canst not speak,
    but thou canst weep.

Is this a worm?   I see thee lie helpless and naked,
     weeping,
And none to answer, none to cherish thee with
     mother's smiles."

The Clod of Clay heard the Worm's voice, and
     raised her pitying head :
She bowed over the weeping infant, and her life
     exhaled
In milky fondness : then on Thel she fixed her
     humble eyes.

" O beauty of the vales of Har ! we live not for
     ourselves.
Thou seest me, the meanest thing, and so I am
     indeed.
My bosom of itself is cold, and of itself is dark ;
But He that loves the lowly pours his oil upon my
     head,
And kisses me, and binds his nuptial bands around
     my breast,
And says : ' Thou mother of my children, I have
     loved thee,

And I have given thee a crown that none can take
  away.'
But how this is, sweet maid, I know not, and I
  cannot know ;
I ponder, and I cannot ponder : yet I live and
  love ! "

The Daughter of Beauty wiped her pitying tears
  with her white veil,
And said : " Alas ! I knew not this, and therefore
  did I weep.
That God would love a worm I knew, and punish
  the evil foot
That wilful bruised its helpless form ; but that he
  cherished it
With milk and oil I never knew, and therefore did
  I weep.
And I complained in the mild air, because I fade
  away,
And lay me down in thy cold bed, and leave my
  shining lot."

" Queen of the vales," the matron Clay answered,
  " I heard thy sighs,

And all thy moans flew o'er my roof, but I have
    called them down.
Wilt thou, O queen, enter my house ? 'Tis given
    thee to enter,
And to return : fear nothing, enter with thy virgin
    feet."

IV.

The eternal gates' terrific Porter lifted the northern
    bar ;
Thel entered in, and saw the secrets of the land
    unknown.
She saw the couches of the dead, and where the
    fibrous root
Of every heart on earth infixes deep its restless
    twists :
A land of sorrows and of tears, where never smile
    was seen.

She wandered in the land of clouds, through valleys
    dark, listening
Dolours and lamentations, wailing oft beside a
    dewy grave.

She stood in silence, listening to the voices of the
 ground,
Till to her own grave-plot she came, and there she
 sat down,
And heard this voice of sorrow breathed from the
 hollow pit.

" Why cannot the ear be closed to its own
 destruction?
Or the glistening eye to the poison of a smile?
Why are eyelids stored with arrows ready
 drawn,
Where a thousand fighting-men in ambush lie,
Or an eye of gifts and graces showering fruits and
 coined gold?
Why a tongue impressed with honey from every
 wind?
Why an ear, a whirlpool fierce to draw creations
 in?
Why a nostril wide inhailing terror, trembling, and
 affright?
Why a tender curb upon the youthful burning
 boy?

Why a little curtain of flesh on the bed of our
    desire ? "

The Virgin started from her seat, and with a
    shriek
Fled back unhindered till she came into the vales
    of Har.

LATER POEMS.

THE CRYSTAL CABINET.

THE maiden caught me in the wild,
   Where I was dancing merrily ;
She put me into her cabinet,
   And locked me up with a golden key.

This cabinet is formed of gold,
   And pearl and crystal shining bright,
And within it opens into a world
   And a little lovely moony night.

Another England there I saw,
   Another London with its Tower,
Another Thames and other hills,
   And another pleasant Surrey bower.

Another maiden like herself,
　　Translucent, lovely, shining clear,
Threefold, each in the other closed—
　　Oh what a pleasant trembling fear !

Oh, what a smile !　A threefold smile
　　Filled me that like a flame I burned ;
I bent to kiss the lovely maid,
　　And found a threefold kiss returned.

I strove to seize the inmost form
　　With ardour fierce and hands of flame,
But burst the crystal cabinet,
　　And like a weeping babe became :

A weeping babe upon the wild,
　　And weeping woman pale reclined,
And in the outward air again
　　I filled with woes the passing wind.

SMILE AND FROWN.

THERE is a smile of Love,
    And there is a smile of Deceit,
And there is a smile of smiles
    In which these two smiles meet.

And there is a frown of Hate,
    And there is a frown of Disdain,
And there is a frown of frowns
    Which you strive to forget in vain,

For it sticks in the heart's deep core
    And it sticks in the deep backbone.
And no smile ever was smiled
    But only one smile alone

(And 'twixt the cradle and grave
    It only once smiled can be),
That when it once is smiled
    There's an end to all misery.

THE LAND OF DREAMS.

" AWAKE, awake, my little boy !
　　　Thou wast thy mother's only joy.
Why dost thou weep in thy gentle sleep ?
Oh, wake ! thy father doth thee keep."

" Oh, what land is the land of dreams ?
What are its mountains and what are its streams ?
Oh, father ! I saw my mother there,
Among the lilies by waters fair.

" Among the lambs clothèd in white,
She walked with her Thomas in sweet delight.
I wept for joy, like a dove I mourn—
Oh, when shall I again return ?"

" Dear child ! I also by pleasant streams
Have wandered all night in the land of dreams ;
But, though calm and warm the waters wide,
I could not get to the other side."

" Father, O father ! what do we hear,
In this land of unbelief and fear ?
The land of dreams is better far,
Above the light of the morning star."

MARY.

SWEET Mary, the first time she ever was there,
  Came into the ball-room among the fair ;
The young men and maidens around her throng,
And these are the words upon every tongue :

" An angel is here from the heavenly climes,
Or again return the golden times ;
Her eyes outshine every brilliant ray,
She opens her lips—'tis the month of May."

Mary moves in soft beauty and conscious delight,
To augment with sweet smiles all the joys of the
    night,
Nor once blushes to own to the rest of the fair
That sweet love and beauty are worthy our care.

In the morning the villagers rose with delight,
And repeated with pleasure the joys of the night,
And Mary arose among friends to be free,
But no friend from henceforward thou, Mary, shalt
    see.

Some said she was proud, some called her a whore,
And some when she passed by shut-to the door ;
A damp cold came o'er her, her blushes all fled,
Her lilies and roses are blighted and shed.

" Oh, why was I born with a different face ?
Why was I not born like this envious race ?
Why did Heaven adorn me with bountiful hand,
And then set me down in an envious land ?

" To be weak as a lamb and smooth as a dove,
And not to raise envy, is called Christian love ;
But, if you raise envy, your merit's to blame
For planting such spite in the weak and the tame.

" I will humble my beauty, I will not dress fine,
I will keep from the ball, and my eyes shall not
    shine ;

And, if any girl's lover forsake her for me,
I'll refuse him my hand, and from envy be free."

She went out in the morning attired plain and neat;
" Proud Mary's gone mad," said the child in the
    street ;
She went out in the morning in plain neat attire,
And came home in the evening bespattered with
    mire.

She trembled and wept, sitting on the bedside,
She forgot it was night, and she trembled and cried;
She forgot it was night, she forgot it was morn,
Her soft memory imprinted with faces of scorn ;

With faces of scorn and with eyes of disdain,
Like foul fiends inhabiting Mary's mild brain ;
She remembers no face like the human divine ;
All faces have envy, sweet Mary, but thine.

And thine is a face of sweet love in despair,
And thine is a face of mild sorrow and care,
And thine is a face of wild terror and fear
'That shall never be quiet till laid on its bier.

AUGURIES OF INNOCENCE.

*T*O *see a world in a grain of sand,*
    And a heaven in a wild flower;
Hold infinity in the palm of your hand,
    And eternity in an hour.

A Robin Redbreast in a cage
Puts all heaven in a rage;
A dove-house filled with doves and pigeons
Shudders hell through all its regions.
A dog starved at his master's gate
Predicts the ruin of the state;
A game-cock clipped and armed for fight
Doth the rising sun affright;
A horse misused upon the road
Calls to Heaven for human blood.
Every wolf's and lion's howl
Raises from hell a human soul;
Each outcry of the hunted hare
A fibre from the brain doth tear;
A skylark wounded on the wing
Doth make a cherub cease to sing.

He who shall hurt the little wren
Shall never be beloved by men ;
He who the ox to wrath has moved
Shall never be by woman loved ;
He who shall train the horse to war
Shall never pass the Polar Bar.
The wanton boy that kills the fly
Shall feel the spider's enmity ;
He who torments the chafer's sprite
Weaves a bower in endless night.
The caterpillar on the leaf
Repeats to thee thy mother's grief ;
The wild deer wandering here and there
Keep the human soul from care :
The lamb misused breeds public strife,
And yet forgives the butcher's knife.
Kill not the moth nor butterfly,
For the last judgment draweth nigh ;
The beggar's dog and widow's cat,
Feed them and thou shalt grow fat.
Every tear from every eye
Becomes a babe in eternity ;
The bleat, the bark, bellow and roar,
Are waves that beat on Heaven's shore.

o

The bat that flits at close of eve
Has left the brain that won't believe ;
The owl that calls upon the night
Speaks the unbeliever's fright.
The gnat that sings his summer's song
Poison gets from Slander's tongue ;
The poison of the snake and newt
Is the sweat of Envy's foot ;
The poison of the honey-bee
Is the artist's jealousy ;
The strongest poison ever known
Came from Cæsar's laurel-crown.

Nought can deform the human race
Like to the armourer's iron brace ;
The soldier armed with sword and gun
Palsied strikes the summer's sun.
When gold and gems adorn the plough,
To peaceful arts shall Envy bow.
The beggar's rags fluttering in air
Do to rags the heavens tear ;
The prince's robes and beggar's rags
Are toadstools on the miser's bags.

One mite wrung from the labourer's hands
Shall buy and sell the miser's lands,
Or, if protected from on high,
Shall that whole nation sell and buy ;
The poor man's farthing is worth more
Then all the gold on Afric's shore.
The whore and gambler, by the state
Licensed, build that nation's fate ;
The harlot's cry from street to street
Shall weave Old England's winding-sheet ;
The winner's shout, the loser's curse,
Shall dance before dead England's hearse.

He who mocks the infant's faith
Shall be mocked in age and death ;
He who shall teach the child to doubt
The rotten grave shall ne'er get out ;
He who respects the infant's faith
Triumphs over hell and death.
The babe is more than swaddling-bands
Throughout all these human lands ;
Tools were made, and born were hands,
Every farmer understands.

The questioner who sits so sly
Shall never know how to reply.
He who replies to words of doubt
Doth put the light of knowledge out ;
A puddle, or the cricket's cry,
Is to doubt a fit reply.
The child's toys and the old man's reasons
Are the fruits of the two seasons.
The emmet's inch and eagle's mile
Make lame philosophy to smile.
A truth that's told with bad intent
Beats all the lies you can invent.
He who doubts from what he sees
Will ne'er believe, do what you please ;
If the sun and moon should doubt,
They'd immediately go out.

Every night and every morn
Some to misery are born ;
Every morn and every night
Some are born to sweet delight ;
Some are born to sweet delight,
Some are born to endless night.

Joy and woe are woven fine,
A clothing for the soul divine ;
Under every grief and pine
Runs a joy with silken twine.
It is right it should be so ;
Man was made for joy and woe ;
And, when this we rightly know,
Safely through the world we go.

We are led to believe a lie
When we see *with* not *through* the eye,
Which was born in a night to perish in a night
When the soul slept in beams of light.
God appears and God is light
To those poor souls who dwell in night :
But doth a human form display
To those who dwell in realms of day.

THE MENTAL TRAVELLER.

I TRAVELLED through a land of men
   A land of men and women too ;
And heard and saw such dreadful things
   As cold earth-wanderers never knew.

For there the babe is born in joy
   That was begotten in dire woe ;
Just as we reap in joy the fruit
   Which we in bitter tears did sow.

And, if the babe is born a boy,
   He's given to a woman old,
Who nails him down upon a rock,
   Catches his shrieks in cups of gold.

She binds iron thorns around his head
   She pierces both his hands and feet,
She cuts his heart out at his side,
   To make it feel both cold and heat.

Her fingers number every nerve
  Just as a miser counts his gold ;
She lives upon his shrieks and cries,
  And she grows young as he grows old.

Till he becomes a bleeding youth,
  And she becomes a virgin bright ;
Then he rends up his manacles,
  And binds her down for his delight.

He plants himself in all her nerves
  Just as a husbandman his mould,
And she becomes his dwelling-place
  And garden fruitful seventyfold.

An aged shadow soon he fades,
  Wandering round an earthly cot,
Full-fillèd all with gems and gold
  Which he by industry had got.

And these are the gems of the human soul,
  The rubies and pearls of a lovesick eye,
The countless gold of the aching heart,
  The martyr's groan and the lover's sigh.

They are his meat, they are his drink;
  He feeds the beggar and the poor;
To the wayfaring traveller
  For ever open is his door.

His grief is their eternal joy,
  They make the roofs and walls to ring;
Till from the fire upon the hearth
  A little female babe doth spring.

And she is all of solid fire
  And gems and gold, that none his hand
Dares stretch to touch her baby form,
  Or wrap her in his swaddling-band.

But she comes to the man she loves,
  If young or old or rich or poor;
They soon drive out the aged host,
  A beggar at another's door.

He wanders weeping far away,
  Until some other take him in;
Oft blind and age-bent, sore distressed,
  Until he can a maiden win.

And, to allay his freezing age,
   The poor man takes her in his arms ;
The cottage fades before his sight,
   The garden and its lovely charms.

The guests are scattered through the land ;
   For the eye altering alters all ;
The senses roll themselves in fear,
   And the flat earth becomes a ball.

The stars, sun, moon, all shrink away,
   A desert vast without a bound,
And nothing left to eat or drink,
   And a dark desert all around.

The honey of her infant lips,
   The bread and wine of her sweet smile,
The wild game of her roving eye,
   Do him to infancy beguile.

For as he eats and drinks he grows
   Younger and younger every day,
And on the desert wild they both
   Wander in terror and dismay.

Like the wild stag she flees away ;
   Her fear plants many a thicket wild,
While he pursues her night and day,
   By various arts of love beguiled ;

By various arts of love and hate,
   Till the wild desert's planted o'er
With labyrinths of wayward love,
   Where roam the lion, wolf, and boar.

Till he becomes a wayward babe,
   And she a weeping woman old ;
Then many a lover wanders here,
   The sun and stars are nearer rolled ;

The trees bring forth sweet ecstasy
   To all who in the desert roam ;
Till many a city there is built,
   And many a pleasant shepherd's home.

But, when they find the frowning babe,
   Terror strikes through the region wide :
They cry—"The babe—the babe is born ! "
   And flee away on every side.

For who dare touch the frowning form,
    His arm is withered to its root :
Bears, lions, wolves, all howling flee,
    And every tree doth shed its fruit.

And none can touch that frowning form
    Except it be a woman old ;
She nails him down upon the rock,
    And all is done as I have told.

WILLIAM BOND.

I WONDER whether the girls are mad,
    And I wonder whether they mean to kill,
And I wonder if William Bond will die,
    For assuredly he is very ill.

He went to church on a May morning,
    Attended by fairies one, two, and three ;
But the angels of Providence drove them away,
    And he returned home in misery.

He went not out to the field nor fold,
　He went not out to the village nor town,
But he came home in a black, black cloud,
　And took to his bed, and there lay down.

And an angel of Providence at his feet,
　And an angel of Providence at his head,
And in the midst a black, black cloud,
　And in the midst the sick man on his bed.

And on his right hand was Mary Green,
　And on his left hand was his sister Jane,
And their tears fell through the black, black cloud
　To drive away the sick man's pain.

" Oh, William if thou dost another love,
　Dost another love better than poor Mary,
Go and take that other to be thy wife,
　And Mary Green shall her servant be."

" Yes, Mary, I do another love,
　Another I love far better than thee,
And another I will have for my wife :
　Then what have I to do with thee ?

" For thou art melancholy pale,
  And on thy head is the cold moon's shine,
But she is ruddy and bright as day,
  And the sunbeams dazzle from her eyne."

Mary trembled, and Mary chilled,
  And Mary fell down on the right-hand floor,
That William Bond and his sister Jane
  Scarce could recover Mary more.

When Mary woke and found her laid
  On the right hand of her William dear,
On the right hand of his loved bed,
  And saw her William Bond so near ;

The fairies that fled from William Bond
  Danced around her shining head ;
They danced over the pillow white,
  And the angels of Providence left the bed.

" I thought Love lived in the hot sunshine,
  But, oh, he lives in the moony light !
I thought to find Love in the heat of day,
  But sweet Love is the comforter of night.

" Seek Love in the pity of others' woe,
  In the gentle relief of another's care,
In the darkness of night and the winter's snow,
  With the naked and outcast—seek Love there."

THE GOLDEN NET.

BENEATH a white-thorn's lovely may,
    Three virgins at the break of day.—
" Whither, young man, whither away ?
Alas for woe ! alas for woe ! "
They cry, and tears for ever flow.
The first was clothed in flames of fire,
The second clothed in iron wire ;
The third was clothed in tears and sighs,
Dazzling bright before my eyes.
They bore a net of golden twine
To hang upon the branches fine.
Pitying, I wept to see the woe
That love and beauty undergo—

To be clothed in burning fires
And in ungratified desires,
And in tears clothed night and day;
It melted all my soul away.
When they saw my tears, a smile
That might heaven itself beguile
Bore the golden net aloft,
As on downy pinions soft,
Over the morning of my day.
Underneath the net I stray,
Now entreating Flaming-fire,
Now entreating Iron-wire,
Now entreating tears-and-sighs.—
Oh, when will the morning rise?

THE GREY MONK.

" I SEE, I see," the Mother said,
    " My children die for lack of bread!
What more has the merciless tyrant said?"
The Monk sat him down on her stony bed.

The blood red ran from the Grey Monk's side,
His hands and feet were wounded wide,
His body bent, his arms and knees
Like to the roots of ancient trees.

His eye was dry, no tear could flow,
A hollow groan bespoke his woe ;
He trembled and shuddered upon the bed ;
At length with a feeble cry he said :

" When God commanded this hand to write
In the shadowy hours of deep midnight,
He told me that all I wrote should prove
The bane of all that on earth I love.

" My brother starved between two walls,
His children's cry my soul appals—
I mocked at the rack and the grinding chain—
My bent body mocks at their torturing pain.

" Thy father drew his sword in the north,
With his thousands strong he is marched forth.
Thy brother hath armed himself in steel,
To revenge the wrongs thy children feel.

" But vain the sword, and vain the bow—
They never can work war's overthrow ;
The hermit's prayer and the widow's tear
Alone can free the world from fear.

" For a tear is an intellectual thing,
And a sigh is the sword of an angel king ;
And the bitter groan of a martyr's woe
Is an arrow from the Almighty's bow."

The hand of vengeance found the bed
To which the purple tyrant fled ;
The iron hand crushed the tyrant's head,
And became a tyrant in his stead.

THE TIGER.

(SECOND VERSION.)

TIGER, Tiger, burning bright,
    In the forests of the night,
What immortal hand or eye
Framed thy fearful symmetry ?

P

In what distant deeps or skies
Burned that fire within thine eyes ?
On what wings dared he aspire ?
What the hand dared seize the fire ?

And what shoulder and what art
Could twist the sinews of thy heart ?
When thy heart began to beat,
What dread hand formed thy dread feet ?

What the hammer, what the chain,
Knit thy strength and forged thy brain ?
What the anvil ?   What dread grasp
Dared thy deadly terrors clasp ?

When the stars threw down their spears,
And watered heaven with their tears,
Did He smile his work to see ?
Did He who made the lamb make thee ?

THE GATES OF PARADISE.

MUTUAL forgiveness of each vice,
    Such are the Gates of Paradise,
Against the Accuser's chief desire,
Who walked among the stones of fire.
Jehovah's fingers wrote the Law :
He wept ; then rose in zeal and awe,
And, in the midst of Sinai's heat,
Hid it beneath His Mercy-Seat.
    O Christians ! Christians ! tell me why
You rear it on your altars high !

THE KEYS OF THE GATES.

THE caterpillar on the leaf
Reminds thee of thy mother's grief.
My Eternal Man set in repose,
The Female from his darkness rose ;
And she found me beneath a tree,
A mandrake, and in her veil hid me.
Serpent reasonings us entice
Of good and evil, virtue, vice.

Doubt self-jealous, watery folly,
Struggling through Earth's melancholy,
Naked in air, in shame, and fear,
Blind in fire, with shield and spear,
Two horrid reasoning cloven fictions,
In doubt which is self-contradiction,
A dark hermaphrodite I stood—
Rational truth, root of evil and good,
Round me, flew the flaming sword ;
Round her, snowy whirlwinds roared,
Freezing her veil, the mundane shell.
I rent the veil where the dead dwell :
When weary man enters his cave,
He meets his Saviour in the grave.
Some find a female garment there,
And some a male, woven with care,
Lest the sexual garments sweet
Should grow a devouring winding-sheet.
One dies! alas! the living and dead!
One is slain, and one is fled !
In vain-glory hatched and nursed,
By double spectres, self-accursed.
My son ! my son ! thou treatest me

But as I have instructed thee.
On the shadows of the moon,
Climbing through night's highest noon :
In Time's ocean falling, drowned :
In aged ignorance profound,
Holy and cold, I clipped the wings
Of all sublunary things :
And in depths of icy dungeons
Closed the father and the sons.
But, when once I did descry
The Immortal Man that cannot die,
Through evening shades I haste away
To close the labours of my day.
The door of Death I open found,
And the worm weaving in the ground :
Thou'rt my mother, from the womb ;
Wife, sister, daughter, to the tomb :
Weaving to dreams the sexual strife,
And weeping over the web of life.

THE BIRDS.

HE.

WHERE thou dwellest, in what grove,
   Tell me, fair one, tell me, love ;
Where thou thy charming nest dost build,
O thou pride of every field !

SHE.

Yonder stands a lonely tree :
There I live and mourn for thee.
Morning drinks my silent tear,
And evening winds my sorrow bear.

HE.

O thou summer's harmony,
I have lived and mourned for thee ;
Each day I moan along the wood,
And night hath heard my sorrows loud.

SHE.

Dost thou truly long for me ?
And am I thus sweet to thee ?
Sorrow now is at an end,
O my lover and **my friend** !

HE.

Come ! on wings of joy we'll fly
To where my bower is hung on high ;
Come, and make thy calm retreat
Among green leaves and blossoms sweet.

DEDICATION OF THE DESIGNS TO BLAIR'S "GRAVE."

TO QUEEN CHARLOTTE.

THE door of Death is made of gold,
   That mortal eyes cannot behold :
But, when the mortal eyes are closed,
And cold and pale the limbs reposed,
The soul awakes, and, wondering, sees
In her mild hand the golden keys.
The grave is heaven's golden gate,
And rich and poor around it wait :
O Shepherdess of England's fold,
Behold this gate of pearl and gold !

To dedicate to England's Queen
The visions that my soul has seen,
And by her kind permission bring
What I have borne on solemn wing
From the vast regions of the grave.
Before her throne my wings I wave,
Bowing before my sovereign's feet.
The Grave produced these blossoms sweet,
In mild repose from earthly strife ;
The blossoms of eternal life.

BROKEN LOVE.

MY Spectre around me night and day
Like a wild beast guards my way ;
My Emanation far within
Weeps incessantly for my sin.

A fathomless and boundless deep,
There we wander, there we weep ;
On the hungry craving wind
My Spectre follows thee behind.

He scents thy footsteps in the snow,
Wheresoever thou dost go ;
Through the wintry hail and rain
When wilt thou return again ?

Poor, pale, pitiable form,
That I follow in a storm,
From sin I never shall be free
Till thou forgive and come to me.

A deep winter, dark and cold,
Within my heart thou dost unfold ;
Iron tears and groans of lead
Thou bind'st around my aching head.

Dost thou not in pride and scorn
Fill with tempests all my morn,
And with jealousies and fears ?
And fill my pleasant nights with tears ?

O'er *my* sins thou dost sit and moan :
Hast thou no sins of thine own ?
O'er *my* sins thou dost sit and weep,
And lull thine own sins fast asleep.

Thy weeping thou shalt ne'er give o'er ;
I sin against thee more and more,
And never will from sin be free
Till thou forgive and come to me.

What transgressions I commit
Are for thy transgressions fit—
They, thy harlots, thou their slave ;
And my bed becomes their grave.

Seven of my sweet loves thy knife
Hath bereavèd of their life :
Their marble tombs I built with tears
And with cold and shadowy fears.

Seven more loves weep night and day
Round the tombs where my loves lay,
And seven more loves attend at night
Around my couch with torches bright.

And seven more loves in my bed
Crown with vine my mournful head ;
Pitying and forgiving all
Thy transgressions, great and small.

When wilt thou return, and view
My loves, and them in life renew ?
When wilt thou return and live ?
When wilt thou pity as I forgive ?

Throughout all eternity
I forgive you, you forgive me.
As our dear Redeemer said :
" This the wine, and this the bread."

YOUNG LOVE.

ARE not the joys of morning sweeter
Than the joys of night ?
And are the vigorous joys of youth
Ashamèd of the light ?

Let age and sickness silent rob
The vineyard in the night ;
But those who burn with vigorous youth
Pluck fruits before the light.

THE TWO SONGS.

I HEARD an Angel singing
  When the day was springing :
" Mercy, pity, and peace,
Are the world's release."

So he sang all day
Over the new-mown hay,
Till the sun went down,
And haycocks looked brown.

I heard a devil curse
Over the heath and the furse :
" Mercy could be no more
If there were nobody poor,
And pity no more could be
If all were happy as ye :
And mutual fear brings peace.
Misery's increase
Are mercy, pity, peace."

At his curse the sun went down,
And the heavens gave a frown.

RICHES.

SINCE all the riches of this world
    May be gifts from the devil and earthly kings,
I should suspect that I worshipped the devil
    If I thanked my God for worldly things.

The countless gold of a merry heart,
    The rubies and pearls of a loving eye,
The idle man never can bring to the mart,
    Nor the cunning hoard up in his treasury.

CUPID.

WHY was Cupid a boy?
    And why a boy was he?
He should have been a girl,
    For aught that I can see.

For he shoots with his bow,
    And the girl shoots with her eye;
And they both are merry and glad,
    And laugh when we do cry.

Then to make Cupid a boy
　　Was surely a woman's plan,
For a boy never learns so much
　　Till he has become a man.

And then he's so pierced with cares,
　　And wounded with arrowy smarts,
That the whole business of his life
　　Is to pick out the heads of the darts.

LOVE'S SECRET.

NEVER seek to tell thy love,
　　Love that never told can be ;
For the gentle wind doth move
　　Silently, invisibly.

I told my love, I told my love,
　　I told her all my heart,
Trembling, cold, in ghastly fears.
　　Ah ! she did depart !

Soon after she was gone from me,
A traveller came by,
Silently, invisibly :
He took her with a sigh.

THE WILD FLOWER'S SONG.

A S I wandered in the forest
The green leaves among,
I heard a wild-flower
Singing a song.

" I slept in the earth
In the silent night ;
I murmured my thoughts,
And I felt delight.

" In the morning I went,
As rosy as morn,
To seek for new joy,
But I met with scorn."

OPPORTUNITY.

HE who bends to himself a joy
　　Does the wingèd life destroy ;
But he who kisses the joy as it flies
Lives in eternity's sunrise.

If you trap the moment before it's ripe,
The tears of repentance you'll certainly wipe ;
But, if once you let the ripe moment go,
You can never wipe off the tears of woe.

SEED-SOWING.

" THOU hast a lapful of seed,
　　And this is a fair country.
Why dost thou not cast thy seed,
　　And live in it merrily ? "

" Shall I cast it on the sand,
And turn it into fruitful land ?
For on no other ground can I sow my seed
Without tearing up some stinking weed."

BARREN BLOSSOM.

I FEARED the fury of my wind
   Would blight all blossoms fair and true
And my sun it shined and shined,
   And my wind it never blew.

But a blossom fair or true
   Was not found on any tree;
For all blossoms grew and grew
   Fruitless, false, though fair to see.

———

NIGHT AND DAY.

SILENT, silent Night,
   Quench the holy light
Of thy torches bright;

For, possessed of Day,
Thousand spirits stray
That sweet joys betray.

Q

Why should joys be sweet
Usèd with deceit,
Nor with sorrows meet?

But an honest joy
Doth itself destroy
For a harlot coy.

———

IN A MYRTLE SHADE.

TO a lovely myrtle bound,
      Blossoms showering all around,
Oh, how weak and weary I
Underneath my myrtle lie!

Why should I be bound to thee,
O my lovely myrtle-tree?
Love, free love, cannot be bound
To any tree that grows on ground.

PROSE EXTRACTS.

The following extracts are from Blake's Illustrated
Catalogue of Pictures.   (Pub. 1809.)

CHAUCER'S CANTERBURY PILGRIMS.

THE time chosen is early morning before sunrise, when the jolly company are just quitting
the Tabarde Inn.   The Knight and Squire, with the
squire's yeomen, lead the procession ; next follow
the youthful Abbess, her Nun, and three Priests.
Her greyhounds attend her ;

> " Of small hounds had she that she fed
>   With roast flesh, milk, and wasted bread."

Next follow the Friar and Monk, then the Tapiser,
the Pardoner, and the Sompnour and Manciple.
After these "Our Host," who occupies the centre of
the cavalcade, directs them to the Knight as the
person who would be likely to commence their
task of each telling a tale in their order.   After
the Host follow the Shipman, the Haberdasher,
the Dyer, the Franklin, the Physician, the Ploughman, the Lawyer, the poor Parson, the Merchant,

the Wife of Bath, the Miller, the Cook, the Oxford
Scholar, Chaucer himself; and the Reeve comes
as Chaucer has described;

 " And ever he rode hinderest of the rout."

These last are issuing from the gateway of
the inn; the Cook and the Wife of Bath are
both taking their morning's draught of comfort.
Spectators stand at the gateway of the inn, and
are composed of an old man, a woman, and
children. The landscape is an eastward view of
the country from the Tabarde Inn, in Southwark,
as it may be supposed to have appeared in
Chaucer's time; interspersed with cottages and
villages. The first beams of the sun are seen
above the horizon; some buildings and spires
indicate the situation of the Great City. The inn
is a Gothic building, which Thynne, in his glossary,
says was the lodging of the Abbot of Hyde, by
Winchester. On the inn is inscribed its title, and
a proper advantage is taken of this circumstance to
describe the subject of the picture. The words
written over the gateway of the inn are as follows
—"The Tabarde Inn, by Henry Baillie, the
lodgynge-house for Pilgrims who journey to St.
Thomas' Shrine at Canterbury." The characters
of Chaucer's Pilgrims are the characters which
compose all ages and nations. As one age falls
another rises, different to mortal sight, but to
immortals only the same; for we see the same
characters repeated again and again, in animals,

vegetables, and minerals, and in men. Nothing
new occurs in identical existence : accident ever
varies, substance can never suffer change or decay.
Of Chaucer's characters, as described in his
" Canterbury Tales," some of the names or titles
are altered by time, but the characters themselves
for ever remain unaltered ; and, consequently, they
are the physiognomies or lineaments of universal
human life, beyond which nature never steps.
Names alter, things never alter. I have known
multitudes of those who would have been monks in
the age of monkery, who in this deistical age are
Deists. As Newton numbered the stars, and as
Linnæus numbered the plants, so Chaucer numbered the classes of men. The painter has consequently varied the heads and forms of his
personages into all nature's varieties ; the horses he
has also varied to accord to their riders ; the
costume is correct according to authentic monuments. The Knight and Squire, with the Squire's
yeomen, lead the procession, as Chaucer has also
placed them first in his prologue. The Knight is a
true hero, a good, great, and wise man. His whole
length portrait on horse-back, as written by
Chaucer, cannot be surpassed. He has spent his
life in the field, has ever been a conqueror, and is
that species of character which in every age stands
as the guardian of man against the oppressor.
His son is like him, with the germ of perhaps
greater perfection still, as he blends literature and
the arts with his warlike studies.

Their dress and their horses are of the first rate, without ostentation, and with all the true grandeur that unaffected simplicity, when in high rank, always displays. The Squire's Yeoman is also a great character, a man perfectly knowing in his profession.

"And in his hand he bare a mighty bow."

Chaucer describes here a mighty man, one who in war is the worthy attendant on noble heroes. The Prioress follows these with her female chaplain—

"Another nonne also with her had she,
That was her chaplain, and priestes three."

This lady is described also as of the first rank, rich and honoured ; she has certain peculiarities and little delicate affectations, not unbecoming in her, being accompanied with what is truly grand and really polite. Her person and face Chaucer has described with minuteness. It is very elegant, and was the beauty of our ancestors till after Elizabeth's time, when voluptuousness and folly began to be accounted beautiful. Her companion and her three priests were no doubt all perfectly delineated in those parts of Chaucer's work which are now lost ; we ought to suppose them suitable attendants on rank and fashion. The Monk follows these with the Friar. The painter has also grouped with these the Pardoner, and the Sompnour, and the Manciple, and has here also introduced one of the rich citizens of London—characters likely to ride in company, all being above the common rank in life or attendants on those who were so. For the Monk is described by Chaucer as a man of the first rank in society, noble, rich, and expensively attended ; he is a leader of the age, with certain humorous accompaniments in his character, that do not degrade, but render him an object of dignified mirth, but also with other accompaniments not so respectable. The Friar is a character also of a mixed kind.

> "A friar there was, a wanton and a merry."

But in his office he is said to be a "full solemn man," eloquent, amorous, witty, and satirical ; young, handsome, and rich ; he is a complete rogue, with constitutional gaiety enough to make him a master of all pleasures of the world—

> "His neck was white as the flowerdelis,
> Thereto strong he was a champioun."

It is necessary here to speak of Chaucer's own character, that I may set certain mistaken critics right in their conception of the humour and fun that occur on the journey. Chaucer is himself the great poetical observer of men, who in every age is born to record and eternise its acts. This he does as a master, as a father and superior, who looks down on their little follies, from the Emperor to the Miller, sometimes with severity, oftener with

joke and sport. Accordingly Chaucer has made
his Monk a great tragedian, one who studied
poetical art. So much so, that the generous
Knight is, in the compassionate dictates of his
soul, compelled to cry out—

> "' Ho,' quoth the Knight 'good sir, no more of this,
> That ye have said is right ynough, I wis.
> And mokell more for little heaviness
> Is right enough for much folk, as I guess.
> I say, for me, it is a great disease,
> Whereas men have been in wealth and ease,
> To heare of their sudden fall, alas !
> And the contrary is joy and solas.'"

The Monk's definition of tragedy in the proem
to his tale is worth repeating—

> " Tragedy is to tell a certain story,
> As olde books us maken memory,
> Of him that stood in great prosperity,
> And be fallen out of high degree
> Into misery and ended wretchedly !"

Though a man of luxury, pride, and pleasure,
he is a master of art and learning, though affecting
to despise it. Those who think that to the proud
Huntsman and noble Housekeeper Chaucer's
Monk is intended for a buffoon or burlesque
character, know little of Chaucer. For the Host
who follows this group and holds the centre of
the cavalcade is a first-rate character, and his jokes
are no trifles ; they are always, though uttered with
audacity, equally free with the Lord and Peasant,

they are always substantially and weightily expressive of knowledge and experience. Henry Baillie, the keeper of the greatest inn of the greatest city—for such was the Tabarde Inn in Southwark, near London—our host, was also a leader of the age. By way of illustration, I instance Shakespeare's witches in "Macbeth." Those who dress them for the stage consider them as wretched old women, and not as Shakespeare intended, the Goddesses of Destiny. This shows how much Chaucer has been misunderstood in his sublime work. Shakespeare's fairies also are the rulers of the vegetable world, and so are Chaucer's. Let them be so considered, and then the poet will be understood, and not else. But I have omitted to speak of a very prominent character, the Pardoner—the Age's Knave—who always commands and domineers over the high and low vulgar. This man is sent in every age for a rod and scourge, and for a blight, for a trial of men, to divide the classes of men ; he is in the most holy sanctuary, and he is suffered by Providence for wise ends, and has also his use, and grand leading destiny.

His companion, the Sompnour, is also a devil of the first magnitude—grand, terrific, rich, and honoured in the rank of which he holds the destiny. The uses to society are perhaps equal of the Devil and of the Angel ; their sublimity who can dispute?

> " In daunger had he at his owne gise,
> The younge girles of his diocese,
> And he knew well their counsel," etc.

The principal figure in the next group is the Good
Parson—an Apostle, a real Messenger of Heaven,
sent in every age for its light and its warmth.
This man is beloved and venerated by all, and
neglected by all : he serves all, and is served by
none. He is, according to Christ's definition, the
greatest of his age ; yet he is a Poor Parson of a
town. Read Chaucer's description of the Good
Parson, and bow the head and knee to Him who,
in every age, sends us such a burning and a shining
light. Search, O ye rich and powerful, for these
men, and obey their counsel ; then shall the
Golden Age return. But alas ! you will not easily
distinguish him from the Friar or the Pardoner ;
they also are "full solemn men," and their counsel
you will continue to follow. I have placed by his
side the Sergeant-at-Lawe, who appears delighted
to ride in his company, and between him and his
brother the Ploughman, as I wish men of law would
always ride with them and take their counsel,
especially in all difficult points. Chaucer's Lawyer
is a character of great venerableness—a judge, and
a real master of the jurisprudence of his age. The
Doctor of Physic is in this group, and the Franklin, the voluptuous country gentleman, contrasted
with the Physician ; and, on his other hand, the
two Citizens of London. Chaucer's characters live
age after age. Every age is a Canterbury Pilgrimage ; we all pass on, each sustaining one or other
of these characters ; nor can a child be born who
is not one of these characters of Chaucer. The

Doctor of Physic is described as the first of his profession—perfect, learned, completely Master and Doctor in his art. Thus the reader will observe that Chaucer makes every one of his characters perfect in his kind; every one is an Antique Statue, the image of a class, and not an imperfect individual. This group also would furnish substantial matter, on which volumes might be written. The Franklin is one who keeps open table, who is the genius of eating and drinking—the Bacchus; as the Doctor of Physic is the Æsculapius, the Host is the Silenus, the Squire is the Apollo, the Miller is Hercules, etc. Chaucer's characters are a description of the eternal principles that exist in all ages. The Franklin is voluptuousness itself most nobly portrayed.

> "It snowed in his house of meat and drink."

The Ploughman is simplicity itself, with wisdom and strength for its stamina. Chaucer has divided the ancient character of Hercules between his Miller and his Ploughman. Benevolence is the Ploughman's great characteristic; he is thin with excessive labour, and not with old age as some have supposed—

> "He woulde thresh and thereto dike and delve,
> For Christe's sake, for every poore wight,
> Withouten hire, if it lay in his might."

Visions of these eternal principles or characters of human life appear to poets in all ages. The Grecian gods were the ancient Cherubim of

Phœnicia; but the Greeks, and since them the Moderns, have neglected to subdue the gods of Priam. These gods are visions of the eternal attributes, or divine names, which, when erected into gods, become destructive to humanity. They ought to be the servants, and not the masters, of man or of society. They ought to be made to sacrifice to man, and not man compelled to sacrifice to them; for, when separated from man or humanity, who is Jesus the Saviour, the vine of eternity? They are thieves and rebels, they are destroyers. The Ploughman of Chaucer is Hercules in his supreme eternal state, divested of his spectrous shadow, which is the Miller, a terrible fellow, such as exists in all times and places, for the trial of men, to astonish every neighbourhood with brutal strength and courage, to get rich and powerful, to curb the pride of man. The Reeve and the Manciple are two characters of the most consummate worldly wisdom. The Shipman or Sailor is a similar genius of Ulyssean art, but with the highest courage superadded. The Citizens and their Cook are each leaders of a class. Chaucer has been somehow made to number four citizens, which would make his whole company, himself included, thirty-one. But he says there were but nine-and-twenty in his company—

"Full nine-and-twenty in a company."

The Webbe, or Weaver, and the Tapiser, or

Tapestry Weaver, appear to me to be the same person ; but this is only an opinion, for full nine-and-twenty may signify one more or less. But I dare say Chaucer wrote "A Webbe Dyer," that is, a Cloth Dyer—

"A Webbe Dyer and a Tapiser."

The merchant cannot be one of the Three Citizens, as his dress is different, and his character is more marked, whereas, Chaucer says of his rich citizens :—

" All were yclothed in o liverie."

The character of woman Chaucer has divided into two classes—the Lady Prioress and the Wife of Bath. Are not these leaders of the ages of men? The Lady Prioress in some ages pre-dominates, and in some the Wife of Bath, in whose character Chaucer has been equally minute and exact, because she is also a scourge and a blight. I shall say no more of her, nor expose what Chancer has left hidden ; let the young reader study what he has said of her—it is useful as a scarecrow. There are of such characters born too many for the peace of the world. I come at length to the Clerk of Oxenford. This character varies from that of Chaucer, as the contemplative philoso-pher varies from the poetical genius. There are always these two classes of learned sages—the poeti-cal and the philosophical. The painter has put

them side by side, as if the youthful clerk had put
himself under the tuition of the mature poet. Let the
philosopher always be the servant and scholar of
inspiration, and all will he happy. Such are the
characters that compose this picture, which was
painted in self-defence against the insolent and
envious imputation of unfitness for finished and
scientific art ; and this imputation most artfully and
industriously endeavoured to be propagated among
the public by ignorant hirelings. The painter
courts comparison with his competitors, who having
received fourteen hundred guineas, and more, from
the profits of his designs in that well-known work,
Designs for Blair's "Grave," have left him to shift for
himself ; while others more obedient to an
employer's opinions and directions are employed,
at a great expense, to produce works in succession
to his by which they acquired public patronage.
This has hitherto been his lot—to get patronage
for others and then to be left and neglected, and
his work, which gained that patronage, cried down
as eccentricity and madness—as unfinished and
neglected by the artist's violent temper ; he is sure
the works now exhibited will give the lie to such
aspersions. Those who say that men are led by
interest are knaves. A knavish character will
often say, Of what interest is it to me to do so
and so ? I answer, Of none at all, but the contrary, as you know well. It is of malice and envy
that you have done this ; hence I am aware of you,
because I know that you act not from interest, but

from malice, even to your own destruction. It is, therefore, become a duty which Mr. B——owes to the public, who have alway recognised him and patronised him, however hidden by artifices, that he should not suffer such things to be done, or be hindered from the publc exhibition of his finished productions by any calumnies in future. The character and expression in this picture could never have been produced with Rubens' light and shadow, or with Rembrandt's, or anything Venetian or Flemish. The Venetian and Flemish practice is broken lines, broken masses, and broken colours. Mr. B——'s practice is unbroken lines, unbroken masses, and unbroken colours. Their art is to lose form ; his art is to find form and to keep it. His arts are opposite to theirs in all things. As there is a class of men whose whole delight is in the destruction of men, so there is a class of artists whose whole art and science is fabricated for this purpose of destroying art. Who these are is soon known ; " by their works ye shall know them." All who endeavour to raise up a style against Raphael, Michael Angelo, and he Antique —those who separate Painting from Drawing ; who look if a picture is well drawn, and, if it is, immediately cry out that it cannot be well coloured— those are the men. But to show the stupidity of this class of men, nothing need be done but to examine my rival's prospectus. The two first characters in Chaucer—the Knight and the Squire —he has put amongst his rabble ; and indeed his prospectus calls the Squire "the fop of Chaucer's age." Now hear Chaucer—

> " Of his stature, he was even length
> And wonderly deliver, and of great strength ;
> And he had be sometime in Chivanchy,
> In Flanders, in Antonis, and in Picardy,
> And borne him well as of so little space."

Was this a fop?

> " Well could he sit a horse, and faire ride.
> He could songs make, and eke well indite,
> Joust, and eke dance, portray, and well wiite."

Was this a fop?

> "Curteis he was, and meek, and serviceable ;
> And kerft before his fader at the table."

Was this a fop?

It is the same with all his characters ; he has done all by chance, or perhap his fortune, money, money. Acording to his prospectus he has Three Monks ; these he cannot find in Chaucer, who has only One Monk, and that no vulgar character as he has endeavoured to make him. When men cannot read, they should not pretend to paint. To be sure Chaucer is a little difficult to him who has only blundered over novels or catchpenny trifles of booksellers ; yet a little pains ought to be taken, even by the ignorant and weak. He has put the Reeve, a vulgar fellow, between his Knight and Squire, as if he was resolved to go contrary in everything to Chaucer, who says of the Reeve—

> " And ever he rode hinderest of the rout."

In this manner he has jumbled his dumb dollies together, and is praised by his equals for it ; for both himself and his friend are equally masters of Chaucer's language. They both think the Wife of Bath is a young, beautiful, blooming damsel ; and H—— says that she is the " Fair Wife of Bath," and that " the Spring appears in her cheeks." Now hear what Chaucer has made her say of herself, who is no modest one—

> " But Lord ! when it remembreth me,
> Upon my youth, and on my jollity,
> It tickleth me about the hearte root,
> Unto this day it doth my hearte boot
> That I have had my world as in my time ;
> But age, alas ! that all will envenime,
> Hath me bereft, my beauty and my pith
> Let go ; farewell ! the devil go therewith !
> The flour is gone, there is no more to tell,
> The bran, as best I can, I now mote sell,
> And yet to be right merry, will I fond
> Now forth to telle of my fourth husband."

She has had four husbands, a fit subject for this Painter ; yet the painter ought to be very much offended with his friend H——, who has called his " a common scene," and " very ordinary forms," which is the truest part of all ; for it is so, and very wretchedly so, indeed. What merit can there be in a picture of which such words are spoken with truth ? But the prospectus says that the Painter has represented Chaucer himself as a knave who thrusts himself among honest people to make game

R

of and laugh at them ; though I must do justice to
the Painter, and say that he has made him look
more like a fool than a knave.   But it appears in
all the writings of Chaucer, and particularly in his
" Canterbury Tales," that he was very devout, and
paid respect to true enthusiastic superstition.   He
has laughed at his knave and fools, as I do now.
But he has respected his True Pilgrims, who are a
majority of his company, and not thrown together
in the random manner that Mr. S—— has done.
Chaucer has nowhere called the Ploughman old—
worn out with "age and labour," as the prospectus
has represented him, and says that the picture has
done so too.   He is worn down with labour, but
not with age.   How spots of brown and yellow,
smeared about at random, can be either young
or old, I cannot see.   It may be an old man ; it
may be a young one ; it may be anything that
the prospectus pleases.   But I know that where
there are no lineaments, there can be no character.
And what connoisseurs call touch, I know by
experience, must be the destruction of all character
and expression, as it is of every lineament.   The
scene of Mr. S——'s picture is by Dulwich Hills,
which was not the way to Canterbury ; but perhaps
the Painter thought he would give them a ride
round about, because they were a burlesque set of
scarecrows not worth any man's respect or care.
But the Painter's thoughts being always upon gold,
he has introduced a character that Chaucer has not
—namely, a Goldsmith, for so the prospectus tells

us. Why he has introduced a Goldsmith, and what is the wit of it, the prospectus does not explain. But it takes care to mention the reserve and modesty of the Painter; this makes a good epigram enough—

" The fox, the mole, the beetle, and the bat,
    By sweet reserve and modesty get fat."

But the prospectus tells us that the Painter has introduced a "Sea-Captain." Chaucer has a Ship-man, a Sailor, a Trading Master of a Vessel, called by courtesy captain, as every master of a boat is ; but this does not make him a sea-captain. Chaucer has purposely omitted such a personage, as it only exists in certain periods : it is the soldier by sea. He who would be a soldier in inland nations, is a sea-captain in commercial nations. All is miscon-ceived, and its misexecution is equal to its misconception. I have no objection to Rubens and Rembrandt being employed, or even to their living in a palace ; but its hall not be at the expense of Raphael or Michael Angelo living in a cottage and in contempt and derision. I have been scorned long enough by these fellows, who owe to me all that they have ; it shall be so no longer.

The Bard, from Gray.

" On a rock, whose haughty brow
  Frowned o'er old Conway's foaming flood,
  Robed in the sable garb of woe,
  With haggard eyes the Poet stood.
  Loose his beard, and hoary hair
  Streamed like a meteor to the troubled air ;
  Weave the warp, and weave the woof,
  The winding-sheet of Edward's race."

WEAVING the winding-sheet of Edward's race by means of sounds of spiritual music, and its accompanying expressions of articulated speech, is a bold, and daring, and most masterly conception, that the public have embraced and approved with avidity.   Poetry consists in these conceptions, and shall Painting be confined to the sordid drudgery of facsimile representations of merely mortal and perishing substances, and not be as poetry and music are, elevated into its own proper sphere of invention and visionary conception? No, it shall not be so!   Painting, as well as poetry and music, exists and exults in immortal thoughts.   If Mr. B——'s Canterbury Pilgrims had been done by any other power than that of the poetic visionary, it would have been as dull as his adversary's. The spirits of the murdered bards assist in weaving the deadly woof ;

" With me in dreadful harmony they join
  And weave, with bloody hands, the tissue of thy line."

The connoisseurs and artists who have made objections to Mr. B——'s mode of representing spirits with real bodies would do well to consider that the Venus, the Minerva, the Jupiter, and Apollo, which they admire in Greek statues, are all of them representations of spiritual existences of gods immortal, to the mortal perishing organ of sight ; and yet they are embodied and organised in solid marble. Mr. B—— requires the same latitudes, and all is well. The Prophets describe what they saw in Vision as real and existing men, whom they saw with their imaginative and immortal organs ; the Apostles the same ; the clearer the organ, the more distinct the object. A Spirit and a Vision are not, as the modern philosophy supposes, a cloudy vapour, or a nothing ; they are organised and minutely articulated beyond all that the mortal and perishing nature can produce. He who does not imagine in stronger and better lineaments, and in stronger and better light, than his perishing mortal eye can see, does not imagine at all. The painter of this work asserts that all his imaginations appear to him infinitely more perfect and more minutely organised, than anything seen by his mortal eye. Spirits are organised men. Moderns wish to draw figures without lines, and with great and heavy shadows ; are not shadows more unmeaning than lines, and more heavy? Oh, who can doubt this ! King Edward and his Queen Eleanor are prostrated, with their horses, at the foot of a rock on which the Bard stands ; prostrated by the terrors of his harp, on the margin of the river Conway, whose waves bear up a corpse of a slaughtered Bard at the foot of the rock. The armies of Edward are seen winding among the mountains—

"He wound with toilsome march his long array."

Mortimer and Gloucester lie spellbound behind their king.

The execution of the picture is also in water-colours, or fresco.

THE ANCIENT BRITONS.

IN the last Battle of King Arthur, only three Britons escaped—these were, the Strongest Man, the Beautifullest Man, and the Ugliest Man. These three marched through the field unsubdued, as gods, and the sun of Britain set, but shall arise again with tenfold splendour when Arthur shall awake from sleep, and resume his dominion over earth and ocean. The three general classes of men who are represented by the most Beautiful, the most Strong, and the most Ugly, could not be represented by any historical facts but those of our own country, the ancient Britons, without violating costume. The Britons (say historians) were naked civilised men, learned, studious, abstruse in thought and contemplation, naked, simple, plain in their acts and manners, wiser than after ages. They were overwhelmed by brutal arms ; all but a small remnant, Strength, Beauty, and Ugliness, escaped the wreck, and remained for ever unsubdued, age after age. The British Antiquities are now in the artist's hands, all his visionary contemplations relating to his own country and its ancient glory, when it was, as it again shall be, the source of learning and inspiration (Arthur was a name for the Constellation Arcturus, or Bootes, the Keeper of the North Pole) and all the fables of Arthur and his Round Table ; of the warlike naked Britons of Merlin ; of Arthur's conquest of the whole world ; of his death or sleep, and promise to return again ; of the Druid monuments or temples ; of the pavement of Watling Street ; of London Stone ; of the caverns in Cornwall, Wales, Derbyshire, and Scotland ; of the Giants of Ireland and Britain ; of the elemental beings, called by us by the general name of Fairies ; and of these three who escaped—namely, Beauty, Strength, and Ugliness. Mr. B—— has on his hand poems of the highest antiquity. Adam was a Druid, and Noah also ; Abraham was called to succeed the Druidical age, which began to turn allegoric and mental signification into corporeal command, whereby human sacrifice would have depopulated the earth. All these things are written in Eden. The Artist is an inhabitant of

that happy country, and if everything goes on as it
has begun, the world of vegetation and generation
may expect to be opened again in heaven, through
Eden as it was in the beginning. The Strong
Man represents the human sublime ; the Beautiful
Man represents the human pathetic, which was in
the wars of Eden divided into male and female ;
the Ugly man represents the human reason. They
were originally one man, who was fourfold ; he
was self-divided, and his real humanity slain on the
stems of generation, and the form of the fourth was
like the Son of God. How he became divided is a
subject of great sublimity and pathos. The artist
has written it under inspiration, and will, if God
please, publish it. It is voluminous, and contains
the ancient history of Britain, and the world of
Satan and of Adam. In the meantime he has
painted this picture, which supposes that in the
reign of that British prince, who lived in the fifth
century, they were remains of those naked heroes
in the Welsh mountains ; they are there now—
Gray saw them in the person of his Bard on
Snowdon ; there they dwell in naked simplicity ;
happy is he who can see and converse with them
above the shadows of generation and death. The
Giant Albion was Patriarch of the Atlantic ; his is
the Atlas of the Greeks, one of those the Greeks
call Titian. The Stories of Arthur are the acts of
Albion applied to a prince of the fifth century, who
conquered Europe, and held the empire of the
world in the dark age, which the Romans never

again recovered. In this picture, believing with
Milton the ancient British history, Mr B—— has
done all as the ancients did, and as all the moderns
who are worthy of fame—given the historical fact
in its poetical vigour, so as it always happens, and
not in that dull way that some historians pretend,
who being weakly organised themselves cannot see
either miracle or prodigy. All is to them a dull
round of probabilities and possibilities; but the
history of all times and places is nothing else but
improbabilities and impossibilities—what we should
say was impossible if we did not see it always
before our eyes. The antiquities of every nation
under heaven are no less sacred than those of the
Jews. They are the same thing, as Jacob Bryant
and all antiquaries have proved. How other antiquities came to be neglected and disbelieved,
while those of the Jews are collected and arranged,
is an inquiry worthy of both antiquarian and
divine. All had originally one language and one
religion; this was the religion of Jesus, the everlasting gospel. Antiquity preaches the gospel of
Jesus. The reasoning historian, turner and twister
of causes and consequences—such as Hume,
Gibbon, and Voltaire—cannot with all his artifice,
turn or twist one fact, or disarrange self-evident
action and reality. Reasons and opinions concerning acts are not history; acts themselves alone
are history, and these are not the exclusive
property of either Hume, Gibbon, or Voltaire,
Echard, Rapin, Plutarch, or Herodotus. Tell me

the acts, O historian, and leave me to reason upon
them as I please ; away with your reasoning and
your rubbish ! All that is not action is not worth
reading. Tell me the What ; I do not want you to
tell me the Why, and the How ; I can find that out
myself as well as you can, and I will not be fooled
by you into opinions that you please to impose, to
disbelieve what you think improbable or impossible. His opinion who does not see spiritual
agency is not worth any man's reading ; he who
rejects a fact because it is improbable must reject
all history, and retain doubts only.

It has been said to the artist, take the Apollo for
the model of your Beautiful Man, and the Hercules
for your Strong Man, and the Dancing Faun for
your Ugly Man. Now he comes to his trial. He
knows what he does is not inferior to the grandest
antiques. Superior it cannot be, for human power
cannot go beyond either what he does or what
they have done ; it is the gift of God, it is inspiration and vision. He had resolved to emulate these
precious remains of antiquity ; he has done so, and
the result you behold his ideas of strength and
beauty have not been greatly different. Poetry as
it exists now on earth in the various remains of
ancient authors, music as it exists in old tunes or
melodies, painting and sculpture as they exist in
the remains of antiquity and in the works of more
modern genius—each is inspiration and cannot be
surpassed : it is perfect and eternal. Milton,
Shakespeare, Michael Angelo, Raphael—the finest

specimens of ancient sculpture, and painting, and architecture, Gothic, Grecian, Hindoo, and Egyptian—are the extent of the human mind. The human mind cannot go beyond the gift of God, the Holy Ghost. To suppose that art can go beyond the finest specimens of art that are now in the world is not knowing what art is ; it is being blind to the gifts of the Spirit.

It will be necessary for the Painter to say something concerning his ideas of Beauty, Strength, and Ugliness. The Beauty that is annexed and appended to folly, is a lamentable accident and error of the mortal and perishing life ; it does but seldom happen, but with this unnatural mixture the sublime Artist can have nothing to do ; it is fit for the burlesque. The Beauty proper for sublime art is lineaments, or forms and features that are capable of being the receptacles of intellect ; accordingly the Painter has given in his Beautiful Man his own ideas of intellectual Beauty. The face and limbs that deviate or alter least, from infancy to old age, are the face and limbs of greatest beauty and perfection. The Ugly, likewise, when accompanied and annexed to imbecility and disease, is a subject for burlesque, and not for historical grandeur. The Artist has imagined his Ugly Man one approaching to the beast in features and form, his forehead small, without frontals, his jaws large, his nose high on the ridge, and narrow his chest, and the stamina of his make comparatively little, and his joints and his extremities large, his eyes with scarce any

whites, narrow and cunning, and everything tending
toward what is truly Ugly—the incapability of
intellect.   The Artist has considered his Strong
Man as a receptacle of Wisdom, a sublime ener-
giser, his features and limbs do not spindle out into
length without strength, nor are they too large and
unwieldy for his brain and bosom.   Strength consists in accumulation of power to the principal seat,
and from thence a regular graduation and subor-
dination ; strength is compactness, not extent nor
bulk.

The Strong Man acts from conscious superiority,
and marches on in fearless dependence on the
divine decrees raging with the inspirations of a
prophetic mind.   The Beautiful Man acts from
duty and anxious solicitude for the fates of those
for whom he combats.   The Ugly Man acts from
love of carnage, and delights in the savage barbari-
ties of war, rushing with sportive precipitation into
the very teeth of the affrighted enemy.

The Roman Soldiers, rolled together in a heap
before them, "like the rolling thing before the
whirlwind," show each a different character and a
different expression of fear, or revenge, or envy, or
blank horror, or amazement, or devout wonder and
unresisting awe.   The dead and dying Britons
naked, mingled with armed Romans, strew the
field beneath.   Among these the last of the Bards
who was capable of attending warlike deeds is seen
falling, outstretched among the dead and dying,
singing to his harp in the pains of death.

Distant among the mountains are Druid Temples similar to Stonehenge. The Sun sets behind the mountains, bloody with the day of battle.

The flush of health is flesh exposed to the open air, nourished by the spirits of forests and floods; in that ancient happy period which history has recorded cannot be the sickly daubs of Titian or Rubens. Where will the copier of nature, as it now is, find a civilised man who has been accustomed to go naked? Imagination only can furnish us with colouring appropriate, such as is found in the Frescoes of Raphael and Michael Angelo; the disposition of forms always directs colouring in works of true art. As to a modern man, stripped from his load of clothing, he is like a dead corpse. Hence Rubens, Titian, Correggio, and all of that class, are like leather and chalk; their men are like leather, and their women like chalk; for the disposition of their forms will not admit of grand colouring. In Mr. B——'s Britons the blood is seen to circulate in their limbs; he defies competition in colouring.

and wiry line of rectitude and certainty in the
actions and intentions? Leave out this line, and
you leave out life itself; all is chaos again, and the
line of the Almighty must be drawn out upon it
before man or beast can exist. Talk no more
then of Correggio, or Rembrandt, or any other
of those plagiaries of Venice or Flanders. They
were but the lame imitators of lines drawn by their
predecessors, and their works prove themselves
contemptible disarranged imitations, and blundering misapplied copies.

THE TRUE AND FALSE IN LITERATURE AND ART.

(From a Public Address.)

WHILE the works of Pope and Dryden are
looked upon as the same art with those of
Shakespeare and Milton; while the works of
Strange and Woolett are looked upon as the same
art with those of Raphael and Albert Durer, there
can be no art in a nation but such as is subservient
to the interest of the monopolising trader.
Englishmen, arouse yourselves from the fatal
slumber into which booksellers and trading dealers
have thrown you, under the artfully propagated
pretence that a translation or a copy of any kind
can be as honourable to a nation as an original,
belieing the English character in that well-known

saying, "Englishmen improve what **others** invent." This even Hogarth's works **prove a** detestable falsehood. No man can improve **an** original invention ; nor **can** an original **invention** exist **without** execution organised, **delineated,** and articulated, either **by** God or **man.** I **do** not mean smoothed **up, and** niggled, **and** poco-pen'd, and all the beauties **paled** out, blurred, and blotted, but drawn **with a** firm **and** decided hand at **once,** like Michael **Angelo,** Shakespeare, **and** Milton. I have heard many people **say,** "Give **me the** ideas, it is no matter what words **you put** them **into,"** and others say, "Give me the **design,** it is no **matter** for the executions." These **people** knew **enough of** artifice, but **nothing** of art. Ideas cannot be given but in their minutely appropriate words, **nor** can **a design be** made without its **minutely** appropriate **execution.** The unorganized **blots** and **blurs of Reubens** and Titian **are not** art, nor **can** their method ever express **ideas or** imaginations, any more than Pope's metaphysical jargon of rhyming. Unappropriate execution is the most nauseous of all affectation **and** foppery. He who copies does not execute ; **he** only imitates what is already executed. Execution is only the result of invention.

OPINIONS.

I.

THE nature of visionary fancy or imagination is very little known, and the eternal nature and permanence of its ever-existent images are considered as less permanent than the things of vegetable and generative nature. Yet the oak dies as well as the lettuce; but its eternal image or individuality never dies, but renews by its seed. Just so the imaginative image returns by the seed of contemplative thought. The writings of the prophets illustrate these conceptions of the visionary fancy by their various sublime and divine images as seen in the worlds of vision.

2.

Aristotle says, characters are either good or bad: now, goodness or badness has nothing to do with character. An apple-tree, a pear-tree, a horse, a lion, are characters; but a good apple-tree or a bad, is an apple-tree still. A horse is not more a lion for being a bad horse—that is its character. Its goodness or badness is another consideration.

3.

Oil has falsely been supposed to give strength to colours; but a little consideration must show the fallacy of this opinion. Oil will not drink or absorb colour enough to stand the test of very little time and of the air. It deadens every colour it is mixed with, at its first mixture, and in a little time becomes a yellow mask over all that it touches. Let the works of modern artists since Ruben's time witness the villainy of some one at that time, who first brought oil painting into general opinion and practice, since which we have never had a picture painted that could show itself by the side of an earlier production. Whether Rubens or Vandyke, or both, were guilty of this villainy is to be inquired in another work on painting, and who first forged the silly story and known falsehood about John of Bruges inventing oil colours. In the meantime let it be observed, that before Vandyke's time, and in his time, all the genuine pictures are on plaster or whiting grounds, and none since.

4.

This subject—an experiment picture—is taken from the visions of Emanuel Swedenborg. The learned who strive to ascend into heaven by means of learning appear to children like dead horses when repelled by the celestial spheres. The works of this visionary are well worthy the attention of painters and poets ; they are foundations for grand things. The reason they have not been more attended to is, because corporeal demons have gained a predominance. Who the leaders of these are will be shown below. Unworthy men, who gain fame among men, continue to govern man-

kind after death, and in their spiritual bodies oppose
the spirits of those who worthily are famous, and as
Swedenborg observes, shut the doors of mind and of
thought by placing learning above inspiration.

5.

The drawing, "The penance of Jane Shore in
Saint Paul's Church," was done above thirty years
ago, and proves to the author, and he thinks will to
any discerning eye, that the productions of our
youth and of our maturer age are not equal in all
essential points. If a man is master of his profession, he cannot be ignorant that he is so ; and if
he is not employed by those who pretend to
encourage art, he will employ himself, and laugh
in secret at the pretences of the ignorant, while he
has every night dropped into his shoe—as soon as
he puts it off, and puts out the candle, and gets into
bed—a reward for the labours of the day, such as
the world cannot give ; and patience and time
await to give him all that the world can give.

6.

All frescoes are as high finished as miniatures
or enamels, and they are known to be unchange-
able ; but oil, being a body itself, will drink or
absorb very little colour, and changing yellow, and
at length brown, destroys every colour it is mixed
with, especially every delicate colour. It turns
every permanent white to a yellow and brown
putty, and has compelled the use of that destroyer
of colour, white lead, which, when its protecting oil

is evaporated, will become lead again. This is an awful thing to say to oil painters ; they may call it madness, but it is true. All the genuine old little pictures, called cabinet pictures, are in fresco and not in oil. Oil was not used except by blundering ignorance till after Vandyke's time ; but the art of fresco painting being lost, oil became a fetter to genius and a dungeon to art. But one convincing proof among many others that these assertions are true is, that real gold and silver cannot be used with oil, as they are in all the old pictures, and in Mr. B——'s frescoes.

7.

Every poem must necessarily be a perfect unity, but why Homer's is peculiarly so I cannot tell. He has told the story of Bellerophon and omitted the Judgment of Paris, which is not only a part, but a principal part of Homer's subject. But when a work has unity, it is as much so in a part as in the whole. The torso is as much a unity as the Laocöön.

8.

The world of imagination is the world of eternity. It is the divine bosom into which we shall all go after the death of the vegetated body. This world of imagination is infinite and eternal, whereas the world of generation, or vegetation, is finite and temporal. There exist in that eternal world the permanent realities of every thing which we see reflected in this vegetable glass of nature.

NOTE.

The Mr. S—— mentioned so often in Extracts was his old friend and rival artist, Mr. Stothard, who had been prompted by Cromek to produce a design of Canterbury Pilgrimage in rival to Blake's own remarkable work. Blake, who believed his old friend to have filched his idea from himself, criticises Mr. Stothard's work in these extracts.—J. S.

PROVERBS.

In seed time learn, in harvest teach, in winter enjoy.

Drive your cart and your plough over the bones of the dead.

The road of excess leads to the palace of wisdom.

Prudence is a rich ugly old maid courted by Incapacity.

The cut worm forgives the plough.

Dip him in the river who loves water.

A fool sees not the same tree that a wise man sees.

He whose face gives no light shall never become a star.

Eternity is in love with the productions of time.

The busy bee has no time for sorrow.

The hours of Folly are measured by the clock, but of Wisdom no clock can measure.

All wholesome food is caught without a net or a trap.

Bring out number, weight, and measure in a year of dearth.

The most sublime act is to set another before you.

If the fool would persist in his folly he would become wise.

Shame is Pride's cloak.

Excess of sorrow laughs ; excess of joy weeps.

The roaring of lions, the howling of wolves, the raging of the stormy sea, and the destructive sword are portions of eternity too great for the eye of man.

The fox condemns the trap, not himself.

Joys impregnate, sorrows bring forth.

Let man wear the fell of the lion, woman the fleece
of the sheep.

The bird a nest, the spider a web, man friendship.

The selfish, smiling fool and the sullen, frowning
fool shall both be thought wise, that they may
be a rod.

What is now proved was once only imagined.

The rat, the mouse, the fox, the rabbit, watch the
roots; the lion, the tiger, the horse, the elephant
the fruits.

The cistern contains, the fountain overflows.

One thought fills immensity.

Always be ready to speak your mind, and a base
man will avoid you.

Everything possible to be believed is an image of
truth.

The eagle never lost so much time as when he
submitted to learn of the crow.

The fox provides for himself, but God provides for
the lion.

He who has suffered you to impose on him knows you.

The tigers of wrath are wiser than horses of in-
struction.

Expect poison from the standing water.

You never know what is enough, unless you know
what is more than enough.

Listen to thefool's reproach ; it is a kingly title !

The eyes of fire ; the nostrils of air ; the mouth of
water ; the beard of earth.

The weak in courage is strong in cunning.

The apple-tree never asks the beech how he shall grow, nor the lion the horse how he shall take his prey.

The thankful receiver bears a plentiful harvest.

If others had not been foolish we should be so.

The soul of sweet delight can never be defiled.

When thou seest an eagle thou seest a portion of genius ; lift up thy head !

One law for the lion and ox is oppression.

To create a little flower is the labour of ages.

Damn braces.   Bless relaxes.

The best wine is the oldest, the best water the newest.

Prayers plough not !   Praises reap not !

Joys laugh not !   Sorrows weep not !

As the air to a bird, or the sea to a fish, so is contempt to the contemptible.

The crow wished everything was black, the owl that everything was white.

Exuberance is beauty.

Improvement makes straight road, but the crooked roads without improvement are roads of genius.

Where man is not, Nature is barren.

Truth can never be told so as to be understood and not be believed.

Enough or too much.

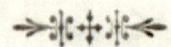

NOTE TO SAMSON (Page 75).

In this poem, which was originally printed as prose, I have followed the example of Mr. W. M. Rosetti in his excellent edition of Blake's Complete Poems, Bell and Daldy, 1874, in printing it as verse, as it is undoubtedly written in metre, though that metre is aught but perfect.   J. S.

WALTER SCOTT, PRINTER,
NEWCASTLE-ON-TYNE.

www.ingramcontent.com/pod-product-compliance
Lightning Source LLC
Chambersburg PA
CBHW021050030726
47496CB00006B/1777